SCORCH

www.chellebliss.com

CHELLE BLISS

USA TODAY BESTSELLING AUTHOR

MEN OF INKED: HEATWAVE SERIES

Same Family. New Love. Next Generation.

Book 1 - Flame (Gigi)
Book 2 - Burn (Gigi)
Book 3 - Wildfire (Tamara)
Book 4 - Blaze (Lily)
Book 5 - Ignite (Tamara)
Book 6 - Spark (Nick)
Book 7 - Ember (Rocco)
Book 8 - Singe - (Carmello)
Book 9 - Ashes (Rosie)
Book 10 - Scorch (Luna)
Book 11 - Torch (Trace)

Learn more at *menofinked.com/heatwave*

SCORCH COPYRIGHT © 2022

Publisher © Chelle Bliss August 2nd 2022
Edited by Lisa A. Hollett
Proofread by Read By Rose
Cover Design © Chelle Bliss
Cover Photo © Eric Battershell Photography
Cover Model: Jonny Kane

www.chellebliss.com
CHELLE BLISS
USA TODAY BESTSELLING AUTHOR

PROLOGUE

IAN

KARMA.

It's something I've never believed in until now.

My past was awful...filled with horrible words and even harsher punishment at the hands of my father.

But I wasn't the only one to suffer. Each of my brothers had the same experience, all of us getting our turn being in my father's cross hairs.

For some people who've experienced repetitive trauma at the hands of someone who's supposed to love them, there comes a point when they eventually fight back.

We hit that day, the breaking point, years ago. Instead of gaining freedom from our abuser, we were imprisoned in another way.

The corrupt criminal justice system in our small town did nothing for years, turning a blind eye to our situation, and once my father was gone, they still showed no mercy.

My brother Nevin took the heat after confessing to causing the death of my father, explaining how it was self-defense. Not just in defense of himself, but the defense of all of us...the Walsh boys.

But no one believed us.

We had been spoken about in whispers since the day we were born. Many in town knew all too well what kind of person my father was, and they did nothing to stop him or rescue us from his clutches.

When Nevin was arrested and eventually put on trial, the whispers morphed into something different. They no longer talked behind our backs, but instead, they made sure we knew how much they disliked "our kind" and how we must've been the children of the devil to do such a horrible thing to our father.

None of us thought Nevin would go to prison. Isn't the system supposed to protect the most vulnerable and the abused? That's what I thought until I saw how the court system really worked.

After he was found guilty, even as a minor, he was given more than a few years of prison time. Not juvie. Not probation. Nevin would go to the place where real criminals lived.

There isn't a day that goes by when I don't think about the hell he must live. It has to be a constant battle to survive, especially at only seventeen and surrounded by full-grown men.

Over the years, he's pulled back, isolating himself from my brothers and me. He stopped calling two years ago. Stopped writing before that. He's refused every visit we've tried to make, saying he wasn't feeling well and to get rid of us.

He shut us out completely.

I haven't laid eyes on him since the day I told him my cancer was in remission. I saw tears in his eyes when he heard the news. His shoulders relaxed, and his entire being seemed to shift when he realized I'd survive.

"Ian," Thomas, my friend Luna's uncle, calls to me, pulling me out of my thoughts. "You ready?"

I nod, running my hands up and down my legs before climbing to my feet. "Thanks for seeing me," I tell him as I walk in his direction with a hand extended.

"I'm always happy to help my family."

The words strike me. I'm not his family. My brother Dylan is by marriage, but not me—at least not technically. But that's how the Gallos are. They're kind people, willing to make their circle bigger, especially for those who have no one to call their kin.

He shakes my hand firmly as he places his palm on my opposite shoulder. "Angel, hold all my calls and ask James to come into my office too."

"Sure thing, love," Angel, his wife, says. Although she's older, she's still one hell of a stunner. The red hair frames her pale skin perfectly, and every feature on her face is beautiful.

3

Thomas steps back, releasing his grip on my hand and shoulder. "Now, what can we do to help you today?"

I take a deep breath, knowing what I have to do, and there's no better time than now. I should've done it years ago, but I made a promise I couldn't break.

But today, I'm finally ready to do what needs to be done to set things straight.

Confess.

1

NEVIN

I BLINK, CONFUSED. "HOW?"

"How what?" my brother Dylan replies.

"How the hell am I out here?" I lift my hands, motioning toward the bright blue sky. "I had time left."

Dylan kicks at the cinders in the prison parking lot, sending them scattering in every direction. "Ian," he breathes.

"What did he do?" I ask as my stomach turns, threatening to spill the contents of my last shitty meal.

I hadn't spoken to a member of my family since I'd found out Ian's cancer had gone into remission. I needed to separate myself from them, leaving behind all the reminders of the freedom and happiness I no longer had.

Ian has struggled with his health for years. I knew he'd never make it on the inside of a prison, and once he went in, the only way he'd get out would be in a body bag. It was why I didn't argue when the cops pinned my dad's death on me. The less they looked, the better chance my brother would have to get treatment and survive.

Dylan tips his face upward, his eyes barely meeting mine. "He confessed."

"What the fuck?" I whisper. "Why? I barely had any time left."

"He did what he thought was right."

"That's bullshit."

"It is what it is."

"It's fucking stupid. What the hell is a month after ten years?"

"He didn't want you to deal with parole, and he wanted your name cleared."

"Fucker," I mutter, trying to control my anger because now my life is fucked, and so is his. "And they just took him at his word?"

Dylan shakes his head. "He brought them the bat that had Dad's blood and Ian's fingerprints on it. He gave them the evidence they never bothered to look for before your trial."

"I want to see him. I didn't do this much time for him to grow a conscience and make a dumbass decision that'll ruin his life."

Dylan grimaces. "You can't."

I stalk toward him, wishing I could punch him square in the face, but I need answers more than revenge. "What do you mean, I can't?

"Why didn't you tell me or anyone?" he asks.

"Tell you what?" I lift my chin, hating my brother more than I have in years. "That I didn't kill our old man?"

"Yeah, man."

"Would it have mattered? What was I supposed to do, let Ian go to jail for protecting the rest of us, where he'd probably die? There was no other decision to be made, Dylan. The only shot Ian had at getting better was to stay out of prison and for me to go in."

"Maybe things would've been different if it had been Ian on trial and not you."

"The justice system is the furthest thing from fair. Shit would've happened the same way with Ian sitting in my seat, except he would've withered away to nothing and died alone. He would've been prey to all the sleazeballs behind bars. I couldn't let it happen. Maybe you should've stuck around and helped protect us from the asshole. Maybe I wouldn't have spent ten years in prison, and Ian wouldn't have had to end his life."

"I couldn't stay. It fucked me up," he admits.

"We were all fucked up," I remind him, knowing exactly how life was and what we did to escape. We did everything and anything. Drugs. Booze. Generally being complete assholes and living up to the horrible reputation we already had. "Now, I'm not going to tell you again—I want to see Ian."

Dylan blows out a loud breath. "You can't."

"Why the fuck do you keep saying that?"

"He's awaiting sentencing," Dylan says, squeezing his eyes shut.

"Fuck," I snap, barely able to breathe. "When? Where?"

"The judge said he'd take into account what led to that moment when determining his sentence. I think he'll go easy on him when he's sentenced next week."

"There's no such thing as going easy on him. Ask me how I know." I glare at my naïve brother.

Dylan scrubs his hand down his face. "Things have changed since you've been inside."

I shake my head. The only thing that's changed is my brother has lost his damn mind. "Yeah. My dumbass brother got a hair up his ass and confessed to a crime I just served ten years for to protect him."

"He needed to do this, Nevin. He needed to set things straight."

I shake my head. "He needed to keep living his life, forgetting I was inside, and keep his damn mouth shut."

"You'll have to talk to him about that."

"Oh. I fucking plan on it."

I fold myself into the seat of his car as he does the same, throwing my few belongings on the floor between my feet. I have nothing to my name except old clothes, a few notebooks, and a couple of family photos I'd hung on my wall to remind me of why I was behind bars instead of Ian.

I always wanted to protect my brothers. If I could take my father's attention away from the others and get beaten instead of them, I did it. Pain was something that went away, but watching them being hurt lasted longer, playing out in my head on repeat.

I stare out the window, watching the trees pass in a blur.

My brother, being my brother and always a pain in the ass, asks, "Why did you shut us out?"

I glance in his direction, staring at his profile as he watches the road. "I did what I needed to do to protect my sanity. As soon as I heard Ian was in remission, I needed to do the last so many years without the constant reminder of everything I would miss. I didn't want to hear about all the great things you guys were doing or the girlfriends you were banging. I needed to create a barrier around myself or else I would've gone mad."

"You sent back every letter we wrote you."

"What I didn't know couldn't hurt me."

"But now you want to know?"

"You still with that uppity Gallo chick?" I ask.

"She's my wife," he hisses.

I jerk my head back, staring at my brother in a new light. "You married a Gallo?"

"Yes, Nev. I married her as soon as she'd have me. She's good people. They're good people. The best family I've ever been around. Nothing like the people who were in our lives."

"I can't believe he married a Gallo," I whisper to myself, turning my face back toward the window and the scenery I haven't set eyes on in what feels like forever.

"They're not like you remember."

"I remember the asshole father always talking shit to us."

"You know we were pricks, though. He had three young girls with his fancy house, and there we were, living like trash and acting worse. Naturally, he'd hate us."

"And now?" I ask him.

"He doesn't treat me any different from his other son-in-law or any member of his family."

"Fucking unbelievable. She must have some magical pussy, brother. Magical fucking pussy."

"Watch it," he warns me.

I bark out a laugh. "Or maybe you're the pussy in the relationship. Or judging by this car, maybe you're a goddamn gold digger."

"I still can and will beat your ass. Doesn't matter that it's your first hour of freedom. You can talk shit about me all you want, but don't say shit about my wife."

"Whatever, Dylan. I don't have to fuck her or deal with her father, so what the hell do I care about that damn family?"

"Ian's grown close to Rosie's twin sister Luna over the years. They're damn near about best friends."

I turned back to him, confused. "Seriously? He's

best friends with pussy who's also a Gallo? What in the actual fuck happened in the last two years?"

He nods. "They're thick as thieves too. She's a good girl. A bit wild, but Ian's not exactly tame either."

"Anyone else hooking up with a Gallo that I need to know about?"

"No."

"Any other women? Anyone else married?"

"No. They like the single life way too much. I think Mom leaving the way she did, when she did, fucked us all up pretty damn bad."

"That ain't no lie."

Only a traitorous, uncaring, selfish bitch would leave her children behind with an abusive man. No one could ever convince me otherwise.

"Did she ever come around while I was inside?"

"Nope. Wherever she went, if she's still alive, she was far enough away that the news must not have found her."

I bark out a laugh. "That's bullshit. She didn't care enough to check on us when we were younger. Why would she bother now? We're nothing to her. Nothing."

"You're probably right," he replies.

"Callum hates her as much as you, me, and Ian, but Finn, Quinn, and Sean are more forgiving when it comes to her. They were too young to realize how much shit changed when she left. She better stay gone. There's no room for her in our world."

"Are you making the decisions for everyone now?" he asks, giving me the side-eye.

"Nah, man, but I'll do what I need to do so her dirt doesn't rub off on anyone else. I won't let her do more damage since she's the only one breathing. We deserve more. We deserve better."

"We don't deserve shit. No one does," he mutters.

"We deserve better than her. There's no doubt about that. We didn't deserve to be beaten on a daily basis, and we certainly didn't deserve to be abandoned by the one parent who showed us a sliver of love. I'll never do that to my kids."

"I promised myself the same thing."

We're silent the rest of the hour-long ride back to the town where life wasn't so beautiful, but it's still a hell of a lot nicer than the prison.

"We're here," he says, parking out front of our old house. "Luna's here, along with the guys and Rosie." He motions toward a truck parked next to us. "Be nice to Luna. She's a good girl, and Ian wouldn't want you to be a dick to her."

"Are they a thing?"

"I already told you they were friends, asshole. Treat her right, or Ian will never forgive you."

"Forgive me?" I laugh. "I just did ten years in the joint for him. I think I'll get a pass."

Dylan shakes his head. "Not when it comes to Luna. She walks on water in his eyes."

I shake my head and grunt. Everyone's gone soft

since I went inside. I no longer understand the people I had been closest to in the world.

Never in a million years would Ian have been best friends with a chick unless he was sticking his dick in her on the regular.

There's a beautiful woman standing on the front porch, waving her hand at us. She's smoking hot in a pair of cutoff shorts and a skintight tank top, showing so much skin my cock is instantly paying attention.

I let out a low, soft whistle.

"Hands and eyes off. That's my wife," he says, waving back at her.

My brother has indeed become a pussy or at least whipped by one, but hell…she's so fucking fine, I'd be her bitch too.

"Relax, man. I haven't seen that much skin on a woman in ten years. I haven't felt the touch of a woman in longer than that. Give me a little bit of a break. I'm not going to try to steal her from you…not yet, at least," I tell him as I slide out of the car and stretch my legs.

"If you want to keep your dick, you'll never make a move on her as long as I'm breathing."

I laugh as we get closer to her, soaking her in. "Calm your bitch ass down, man. She ain't my type."

"I don't remember you having a type."

"Uppity bitches are not it," I inform him.

He stops walking and spins around, pinning me with his eyes and getting in my face. "Call her a bitch one more time, and I'll…"

I lift my hands, not looking for a fight right now. "Hey. No offense. The guys inside didn't call them anything else. I'm going to have to adjust my language along with everything else. I've been out for a little more than an hour. Cut me a little fucking slack."

"I'll give you some slack, but the women around me...they won't. Watch your words."

"They're chicks, Dylan. I'm not scared of them."

He laughs. "They're wicked in ways you could never imagine. Don't underestimate them because they don't have dicks, brother."

I walk behind Dylan as he greets Rosie with a kiss.

"Nevin," she says, turning her beautiful, big blue eyes my way before opening her arms. "We hug in this family."

Normally, I'd grumble, but she looks too delicious not to hug. I am all about whatever she is offering, and the fact that it would piss off Dylan makes it even more appealing.

Fuck him.

"It's so nice to see you again, Rosie. You're all grown up, and I see you've made a man out of my brother."

She slides her arms around me and plasters her breasts against my chest, almost giving me wood. "We're happy to have you back and safe," she says, acting like she doesn't feel my hard length pressed against her stomach. "Our home is your home now."

"Thank you," I tell her, and I can see the attraction

my brother has to her warmth, something we never had any of growing up. "You're too kind."

"It's what family does, silly. You're my family now too," she says softly and finally unwraps her arms from my body. When I turn my head, my brother's watching with a scowl.

"You get enough?" he asks.

Rosie slaps his arm. "Cut it out, Dylan. The man has been surrounded by stinky men for years. I'm pretty sure if an old woman hugged him right now, he'd be just as excited. And anyway, Nevin's going through a lot of feelings at the moment, which he probably doesn't know how to process."

"You're ridiculous," Dylan tells his wife. "Don't let your guard down around him. He's not innocent."

I push down the sudden rush of anger I have toward my brother again. He sets me off, never willing to give me the benefit of the doubt. You'd think after my doing time for Ian, he'd look at me as something more than a piece of shit. "I do know how to control myself, asshole," I remind him. "I'm not an animal."

"Be nice," Dylan's wife chastises him, and I'm loving every minute of it.

He grumbles under his breath while throwing me a killer glare.

"Luna!" Rosie yells with her body twisted toward the screen door. "Nevin's here."

I ready myself, figuring if Ian has this chick as a best friend, she must have something physically wrong

15

with her. Ian didn't do friends with tits, but if he did, she'd have to be the type he never wanted to ever stick his dick in.

But when the screen door opens and a long, curvy leg comes out, nothing can prepare me for the rest.

Holy fucking shit.

Mint doesn't even begin to describe the girl. Her sandy blond hair hangs over her bare shoulder, clinging to her breasts the same way my hands would if given half the chance.

Her big blue eyes and high cheekbones would look even more impressive if her full lips were wrapped around my...

"Jagoff. You going to say hi?" My brother interrupts my thoughts, followed by a backhand to the stomach.

"Hi," Luna says, coming to a stop in front of me. "I'm Luna." She extends her hand to me, not offering me a hug like her twin sister.

I nod. "I remember."

Her gaze moves from my face, down my body, and comes back the same way, but slower. "Not what I was expecting," she says, not looking the least bit impressed with my thrift store outfit.

"Sorry I didn't have time to stop by the mall and grab something different. Prison threads," I inform her, not giving two shits if she likes what I'm wearing or not. "You'll have to deal with it, babe."

"Yep," she mutters, scrunching her nose. "He's exactly how Ian described him."

I drop my few belongings in a busted-up chair nearby. "Not prettier than he said I was?"

She snorts and shakes her head. "Pretty? He said you were an asshole."

I shrug. "Family trait."

"No lie there," she says, still laughing as she looks over at Dylan. "Ian can be an asshole too."

"There was a time when Ian was the biggest asshole out of all of us," I tell her, hating that I'm speaking badly about him when he's not here to defend himself. But then I remember he told her that I was an asshole while I was rotting away in a prison cell to save his life. "Someone as pretty as you would've never given him the time of day back then."

"I'm guessing you two switched on more than your location, then."

"Babe, I'm not an asshole. I'm bitter. They're different."

She takes a step forward, and I stand there like an idiot, unsure of what to do. Before I have a chance to react, she hooks her arm with mine and starts hauling me toward the house.

"Want a beer or something stronger?" she asks.

My brain is buzzing, totally on overdrive as her body touches mine. "Stronger," I croak, barely getting the words out of my mouth.

"Jack, it is," she tells me, pulling me closer to her side, plastering her breasts against my arm.

Fuck.

She smells good. Better than anything my nose has been near in far too long. If you ask me what freedom smells like, I'd describe Luna Gallo, and that shit irks me to no end.

"You're stuck with me," she says as I step foot into the house where the worst shit of my life happened.

You'd think prison was bad, but growing up with my father was a fate worse than anything that happened behind bars.

My stomach twists as I soak in my surroundings, remembering all the painful shit that took place under this roof. The furniture has changed, but the memories can't be wiped out that easily...at least not for me.

"On the rocks?" she asks, leaving me in front of a stool near the counter. "Or straight?"

"One of each."

She nods, going to work in the kitchen like she's been here a million times.

"I'm going to see Ian in a few days if you want to come," she says as she pulls down glasses from the cabinet. "He said he didn't want visitors, but I'm sure you have things to say to him just like I do."

I stare at her ass, unable to stop myself as she grabs two more glasses from higher up. The way her calves harden as she stands on her tiptoes...damn.

"Yeah. I'll go," I say, but my voice is hoarser than normal.

She spins around, smiling at me. "Get a good look?" she asks, clearly taunting me.

I place my arms on the counter and lean forward, giving her a once-over with my eyes. "Could've been longer and with fewer clothes, but it'll do."

She sets down a glass in front of me before reaching for the bottle. "It'll have to do because you don't know it yet, but you're about to have a new best friend, and I already know you think dick and tits don't have friendships."

I almost choke on my own spit at her candor. "Who told you that shit?"

"Ian," she says, pouring some of the Jack into the glass. "He told me everything."

I wrap my hands around the cool glass but keep my gaze pinned on her bottomless blue eyes. "You know that's what he thought, right? Not me."

"He said you'd say that too." She smiles.

"I was barely eighteen when I went away. I'm not the same man I was then."

"I'd argue you weren't really a man then either."

"I was a dumbass kid."

She nods. "But now, you have no excuse."

"No excuse for what?"

"Being an asshole."

"Is there a new law about assholes?"

She giggles and reaches her hand over the counter, touching my wrist. "No laws on the books, but I have a strict no-asshole policy."

Rosie bursts into laughter. "What in the heck are you talking about, Lu? You're an asshole magnet."

19

Perfect. My odds are getting better with every passing moment. Maybe I'll get lucky without much effort on my part.

Luna pulls her hand back, breaking the brief contact she had with me. "I've sworn off them, along with sex. I gave them up for Lent," she tells her sister.

"It's fall."

Luna shrugs. "So?"

"Lent was six months ago."

Luna pours herself a glass of Jack, one bigger than mine. "I'm putting in the work in advance for next year."

"You're ridiculous."

"I'm smart," Luna tells her as she lifts her glass between us and stares at me.

I almost forget how to do normal human shit. I raise my glass, clinking it against hers. "To new friendships," I tell her with a wink.

I could pretend to be a good guy. I'd do it for however long it takes to get a taste of Luna Gallo.

"To new best friends," she corrects me, not dropping her smile for a second. "We're going to have the time of your life."

"Not hard to beat the first twentysomething years, babe."

"Whatever," she mutters before downing the Jack in a single swallow.

I watch her like it's the most erotic thing I've ever seen, and I realize I need to get a fucking grip. A chick like Luna Gallo isn't about to get on her knees for someone who spent ten years in prison.

She is a mere cocktease, thanks to my fucking brother ensuring she makes me her own personal mission.

Ian and I are going to have words about so many things, especially Luna Gallo.

2

LUNA

"This place is depressing," I say to Nevin as we sit in the waiting room of the local jail. And when I say waiting room, I'm using that term as loosely as possible. The chairs are stained and torn, the linoleum tile is dingy and worn, and the walls are a putrid green. It's definitely not a place you want to stay in for very long, but I figure that's how they want it.

Nevin hasn't stopped fidgeting since we walked through the door. He's completely on edge, which is understandable, given his life for the last ten years.

Nevin glances at me as he leans over his legs, elbows on his knees. "Trust me, it's more depressing on the other side. This is like a five-star hotel compared to where Ian is."

"I wish we could break him out," I whisper, trying to ignore the people around us.

"I wouldn't say that too loud."

I cross my arms as I slink down in my chair, unable to wipe the sour look off my face. "They should just let him out. It's not like he's a danger to society."

"They don't care, Luna. They only see him as a criminal. He did the crime, and now he has to do the time."

"He was defending himself and all of you. The judge has to take that into account."

Nevin lifts a shoulder, looking no happier than me. "Don't hold your breath."

"Walsh," a woman calls out from behind the glass.

Nevin's on his feet as soon as he hears his name, leaving me behind. I keep my gaze trained on Nevin instead of the people who are sprinkled throughout the small space.

I try to hear what the woman is saying as Nevin leans against the counter, but I can't hear a damn thing above the voice of the woman who's sitting two seats away.

"It was only a small amount of coke. This is bull-shit," the woman says to another woman who may or may not be there with her. "They should give him a break."

"It's his third time, Molly. He already got two breaks and blew it. You better be prepared for him to be gone for a long, long time," the woman next to her says, not even looking up from her phone. "You're going to be an old bitch by the time he sees the light of day again."

"I can't stick around forever," Molly says back.

"You should've moved on years ago. No one needs a deadbeat like him sticking around. His arrest is the best thing that could've ever happened to you."

"I know," Molly mutters. "I just..." She sighs. "I love him."

"He doesn't love you, babe. See him today and then cut ties," her friend says as if they're talking about a trip to the mall. "It's time to cut ties. Clean break. Got me?"

Molly nods and slumps forward. "I don't know how to do it, but I don't think I can until they sentence him."

"Visit with him today and maybe send him a goodbye letter after he finds out how much time he's getting."

"His court-appointed attorney says ten years minimum, but most likely, he's getting more."

I feel bad for listening to their conversation, but I can't stop myself. Whoever he is, he's going to be pissed, but there's no better time to say goodbye than when you don't have to face the guy for years. And her friend is right; she should've dumped his ass before any of this shit went down.

Nevin stalks back to the chair next to me and collapses into the seat. "A few more minutes, but shockingly enough, they're letting us go in together."

My eyes widen. "They are?"

Nevin nods. "Some shit about your uncle calling in a favor."

I smile, forgetting where I am for a second, thankful to my uncle for making the double visit possible. "It's helpful to have friends or family with connections."

"I wish he'd call in a favor for the sentencing," Nevin says, immediately going back to fidgeting.

I place my hand on his knee, hoping to help calm his nerves. "I can ask."

Nevin shakes his head, but he does nothing to push my hand away. "Don't. A favor for visitation is very different from sentencing, Luna. I don't need to owe your uncle anything."

"He'd never expect you to owe him anything. And anyway, I'd be the one to ask him, so I'd owe him."

"Absolutely not." He stares at me.

"Why?" I stare back.

"Ian wouldn't want it."

"We'll ask him."

"Babe, I know my brother. And since he knows your family, he isn't going to ask for any special favors."

"You don't know your brother as well as you think you do," I tell him, pulling my hand away from his leg. "He's not the same kid you knew, Nevin."

"You think you know him better?"

"I am his best friend," I argue, ready to dig in my heels.

"Walsh," the woman behind the glass says again.

Nevin grumbles as he pushes himself up.

"Should I come?" I ask him.

"Fuck if I know," he says.

I don't bother moving. Nothing is fast here. We're

on their time, and they know we're not going anywhere, no matter how long we have to wait. They're not putting themselves out for someone they think of as the worst part of society.

Nevin talks to the woman and glances back at me with an unreadable look on his face. I haven't figured out how to distinguish between him being happy or annoyed because they're so damn close to the same.

He turns back to her, and I wait, staring at them both as they chat. The woman tips her head toward the orange metal door on the other side of the room.

"Lu, we're up," he says, turning his back on the glass wall barrier and ticking his head to the door just like the woman did. "Let's go."

I scramble to my feet, crossing the room and following Nevin to the door. He has two badges in his hand that state "Visitor" on them. When the door swings open, he hands me one, and I hold it up before clipping it to the collar of my shirt.

I shake my hands, trying to work out my nervous energy before I see Ian. It's been weeks since I've laid eyes on him or even heard his voice. Each step feels like a mile as I follow Nevin and the guard down the narrow hallway.

We're brought into a large room filled with round tables. Prisoners wearing orange are sitting at the tables, surrounded by a visitor or two.

This room sucks even worse than the waiting room. Who knew that was even possible? But somehow, they pulled it off with flying colors. If criminal depression were a design aesthetic, they nailed the hell out of it.

"They'll bring him in. Sit," Nevin says to me when I freeze, soaking in everything about the room.

I don't bother arguing as my ass drops into a seat.

"I've been in this room before, but on the other side," he tells me, taking the seat next to me. "It's less depressing when you're in orange."

I gape at him. "How is that even possible?"

"Because you're so happy to see a friendly face."

My heart sinks as I think about Ian being happy about coming to this room. He doesn't deserve this. He deserved better. They all did.

As the door to the room swings open, my heart almost stops in my chest. Ian's face comes into view. His hair is a mess, sloppy and hanging over his eyes. He has leg chains and handcuffs hanging from his body, which is covered in the same orange jumpsuit as the other people.

"Ian," I whisper, choking back the tears I promised myself I wouldn't shed. What a dumbass I was to think I wouldn't cry when I saw him this way.

Maybe the reality didn't hit me, or I lied to myself, thinking this moment would be so different.

His face is covered by dark hair, and he's clearly given up on shaving. He's skinnier than he was the day he said goodbye. Only a few pounds, but when someone is as thin as he was to begin with, any weight loss is noticeable.

Ian's face brightens as soon as his gaze lands on us. He walks a little taller and lighter than he did when he first stepped through the door.

I want to run to him, throw my arms around his thin frame, and tell him how much I've missed him. I start to stand, but Nevin grabs my forearm, holding me still.

"Don't," Nevin commands.

I glare at him, wanting to rip my arm out of his grasp, but I don't want to jeopardize my time with Ian.

"They'll kick you out."

I curl my fist, holding back my anger. I'm not mad at Nevin. He's trying to do right by Ian and me, but it doesn't make it easier to swallow. He's the only one I can be mad at, and it's not fair of me at all either.

"Nev. Lu," Ian says softly as he sits down, and the guard attaches his handcuffs to the table like somehow he's going to escape. "God, I'm so happy to see your faces."

"Brother," Nevin whispers, his voice cracking. "You look like…"

It's the first bit of emotion I've heard come out of Nevin that isn't snark or anger.

"Don't say 'shit,'" Ian tells him, somehow laughing. "No other way to look in here, but you know that."

Nevin nods, holding his words inside.

"You look good, Ian," I say, somehow not crying like a baby when he turns his gaze totally on me.

"You're not a good liar, Luna." He smiles, and my

inside melt. For the first time in weeks, things almost feel normal, but it's hard to forget where we are.

"No. Really. You don't look as bad as I thought you would," I say, instantly biting my tongue. I'm a complete idiot. That wasn't a nice thing to say, but I said it. I can't take it back.

Thankfully, Ian laughs again. "I missed you, babe."

"Missed you too," I whisper, not able to say it any louder because my throat's starting to close as my nose itches.

Fuck. Do not cry. Do not sob. Hold it together for him, Luna. He's probably miserable enough. He doesn't need to see you cry like a freaking baby.

I take a deep breath, reminding myself I'm here to bring him joy, not my depression.

"Are you doing okay?" Nevin asks him.

"I'm fine. I've been better, but I'm all right."

Nevin blows out a breath, looking mildly relieved.

"Are they treating you okay?" I ask Ian.

"I've definitely been treated worse," Ian replies, and I know he's talking about his father.

Nevin places his arms on the table, leaning forward. "You should've kept your mouth shut. I was close to being out. What the hell were you thinking, Ian?"

Ian glances down before bringing his gaze back to his brother. "I should've gone in to begin with. I never should've let you go in my place. I already stole ten years of your life. I didn't want my actions to follow you forever."

Nevin shakes his head. "That's bullshit. Your ass would be dead if I didn't do it. It was worth every day in prison as long as I knew you were okay. You should've kept your mouth shut."

"I am okay with everything," Ian tells him, adjusting in his seat.

Nevin growls as his eyes darken. "No one behind bars is okay."

"Are you coming to the sentencing?" Ian asks me, ignoring his brother.

I nod. "I planned on it."

"I think you should skip it," Ian says, twisting his wrists in the handcuffs.

I rock back as if he's hit me. "What? Why?"

Nevin grunts, changing up his noises at least. "I agree."

I turn to Nevin, narrowing my eyes as I lift my chin. "I didn't ask you."

Ian laughs. "I miss your attitude, Lu, but Nevin's right."

"No, he's not. I'm coming to hear what the judge says."

Ian frowns and closes his eyes. "I don't want anyone there. Not even you, Nevin," he says, but with his eyes open and trained on his brother. "I want to do it alone."

"Not happening," Nevin mutters. "The guys and I will be there to speak on your behalf. You're not doing this alone."

"I'll be there too," I promise, not taking no for an answer.

"Fuck," Ian grumbles. "It's already going to be hard enough. I don't think I can look at your faces that day."

Nevin slides his hand forward but moves it back in front of him as a guard takes a step toward us. "I get it. Trust me, I do. But you need us there. You just don't know it yet."

Ian leans over the table and brushes his hair away from his forehead. He doesn't reply at first, maybe thinking over what Nevin's said.

"Believe me, Ian. I've been in your shoes."

Ian straightens again and stares at his brother. "I know. I was there. I remember how shitty it was for me to watch them take you away, Nev. I don't want that for you. I don't want that for the guys. And I certainly don't want that for Luna."

I blink, tilting my head like I must've heard him wrong. "Want to repeat that?"

"You shouldn't be there, Luna," Ian states again.

"I don't know when you thought you became the boss of me, Ian Walsh, but I'm going to be there to support my friend, and there's no way you're going to stop me."

"Babe, you think this place is depressing, go to court at sentencing. Nothing more soul-crushing than that," Nevin says, taking Ian's side.

"Are you going?" I shoot back at Nevin.

"Of course, but he's my brother."

"He's my best friend," I throw at him. "And friends are always there for each other."

He drags his hand down his face, muttering behind his palm, "Impossible."

"I don't want this for you," Ian tells me.

I wave a hand around the room. "I don't want this for you either."

"Listen to me," Ian says, scooting closer to the table. "I only have a few more minutes."

My heart sinks. How do we only have a few minutes left? We just got here. We waited longer in the waiting room than we've had Ian with us. It's not fair. Nothing about this is right.

"Whatever happens at the sentencing, I need you to be there for each other," Ian begs. "Nevin needs help figuring out what the hell happened the last ten years."

"Like hell I do," Nevin interrupts, but he stops when Ian glares at him.

"And Nevin, Luna will need someone to look out for her and her questionable choices."

"I do not," I say, giving him the same glare he just gave his brother. "I'm more than capable."

"My time will be easier if I know you two have each other to lean on," Ian adds. "I have enough shit to worry about than to think about you two out there, twisting in the wind."

"I'm not twisting in anything," I tell Ian, fighting back all the emotions that resemble any form of sadness.

"Promise me, Lu. Promise me you'll look after Nevin. He needs someone like you in his life."

Nevin grunts his dissatisfaction with that statement and points at himself. "He's right here, and he's more than capable of taking care of himself."

"You also have the ability to shut out the entire world when the thing you need the most is people. And not just any people, but people who are going to treat you right, brother," Ian explains. "Promise me you'll be there for each other." Ian stares at us, his eyes moving from Nevin to me and back.

"I promise," I mumble, hating that we're here and he's asking something like this of me because he won't be around.

"Me too," Nevin adds with very little enthusiasm.

"Don't do your usual and shut her out, Nev. She's good people, and you could use a little of that in your life right now."

"I love you, Ian," I say, wishing I could give him a hug.

"Love you too, Lu. Don't worry about me. I've got this. Easy peasy."

"Said no one ever about doing time," Nevin tells him.

"Keep her safe…especially from her own reckless decisions," Ian tells Nevin as the guard walks in our direction with a set of keys in his hand.

"Could you be any more dramatic?" I ask Ian, rolling my eyes.

"I could, but I won't," Ian replies, keeping a sense of humor when he's surrounded by so much bad.

"I'll look out for her, Ian."

"And yourself." Ian smiles at his brother. "I love you, Nev. You'd better be good when I get out. We have a lot of time to make up for."

"I'll be waiting," Nevin tells him.

"Time's up," the guard says, and no one argues.

"Bye, Ian," I whisper, choking back the tears that are threatening to fall again.

"Chin up, brother," Nevin tells him.

"Love you guys," Ian replies as the guard unclips his cuffs from the table, hauling him away from us.

My heart sinks as Ian shuffles toward the door. I don't know how long it'll be until I'm this close to him again. A few years ago, we weren't even friends. But now, he's the one I go to when I need solid advice without it becoming public knowledge in my family. He knows how to keep his mouth shut, which is something I never had before...not even with Rosie.

I stare at Ian's back, waiting for him to turn around.

Look at me one more time.

But when the door opens, Ian keeps his back to us, slipping through to the other side, and disappears.

"Fuck," Nevin mutters. "This shit isn't right."

"It's not," I say, unable to blink or process what's going to happen next. "Maybe I should talk to my uncles."

Nevin's hand is back on my arm a second later, but

the contact barely registers. "Don't. Leave it be. Ian wouldn't want that."

"Fine," I snap as I get up from the table, done with this awful place, "But shit better not go wrong."

"It's prison, Lu. Nothing goes right."

3

NEVIN

"WHAT DO YOU THINK IS GOING TO HAPPEN?" FINN ASKS as he sits next to me, wearing his best suit. "Think the judge will go easy on him?"

I turn my head to the side, staring at my brother. I don't want to tell him it's a stupid question, but it is a stupid question. When does anyone, especially someone from law enforcement or the court, ever go easy on a Walsh? "We'll find out soon enough," I tell him, not having the heart to be a complete dick.

Dylan, Rosie, and Luna appear at my side, taking the last three empty seats in our row. Luna sits next to me along with Sean and Quinn, making it a double whammy of chatterers flanking me. Dylan and I give each other a chin lift before he settles in with his wife.

"Hey," Luna whispers, smoothing out her black skirt.

"Hey," I say back, turning my face back toward the front of the courtroom.

She leans over, her shoulder touching my arm. "What's going to happen today? Will we get to talk to him?"

I shake my head and peer down at her. She looks so hopeful, and I hate that I have to kill her positive vibes. "No. The judge will talk, maybe he'll let us talk too, and then Ian'll be sentenced and taken away."

"No last hug?" She chews on the corner of her lip as her eyebrows pull down and in.

"No hugs, Lu. No touching at all."

"I don't know how you did it," she says, shaking her head.

"Didn't have a choice," I tell her.

"Are you going to speak today?" she asks me as everyone around us talks in hushed tones.

I shrug. "If the judge allows me to, but I worry I'm too tied up in this case for my word to mean much."

She reaches over and takes my hand. "Your word means a lot to Ian, and I'm sure the judge will listen to you."

I like her optimism, even if it's naïve. "I doubt they even listen to a word, Luna."

"You have to at least try," she says.

"I will."

The judge walks into the room, followed by Ian being escorted in through another door. His hands and feet are bound just like they were when Luna and I visited him. My brothers are stunned into silence seeing him like that for the first time.

Ian smiles when his eyes land on us. No matter what he said, I know how I felt on the other side of this experience. Having the people you love around you means the world on one of your darkest days.

The sentencing starts like they always do...well, at exactly how mine did ten years ago. The judge talks, and we hang on every word as if somehow he's going to say something different.

"This case is filled with special circumstances," the judge states, giving everyone hope when there isn't any.

Even though I served time, I know it won't be taken into account when determining Ian's sentence. Neither will the fact that he overcame cancer, fighting an enemy he couldn't see.

I drown out the judge, focusing on Ian as he stands next to his lawyer, swaying slightly. He's nervous. I was too. I thought I'd throw up, but somehow I kept it down until I was back in my cell.

Luna elbows me. "You going?"

I blink, focusing on the judge as he stares out across the courtroom.

"He's waiting," she tells me.

I grab the back of the seat in front of me and pull myself to my feet. The judge stares me down as I shuffle forward. Ian turns his head, and his eyes meet mine, making my heart sink and my gut twist. Other people in my shoes would feel bad because of the unknown, but my sorrow comes from knowing too much about what Ian's about to go through.

I stand to the side of the table where Ian and his attorney sit and clear my throat. The judge looks up, dropping his pen as he leans back in his leather chair.

I swallow, ignoring the sandpaper in my throat. This throws me right back to a decade ago when I begged the judge for my life, asking for him to be merciful. Each of my brothers did the same, and each of us was ignored and written off as a punk-ass kid who didn't seem to grasp the gravity of the crime.

"Your honor." I pause and glance to my right, looking at Ian, pushing away any feelings I have of running as I unfold my written statement I spent hours crafting. "I'm here to talk to you about my brother Ian and to beg the court to take into account all he has been through, along with our entire family, for over a decade."

I turn my gaze back to the judge, who's watching while he chews on an arm of his prescription eyeglasses. "Nothing about our life has been easy. We witnessed the daily physical abuse our mother endured since we were little. When our mother couldn't take it anymore, she left us behind with the man who had laid hands on her for years. But she never thought about us or realized his hatred would turn to a new target…us. Maybe she didn't care. Lord knows he never cared about us either."

I reach for a bottle of water that's on the podium and take a large gulp to clear my mind and stop myself from getting too emotional. I've tried to forget the awful times in our house, blocking them out the best I could. But they always find a way back in. Talking about our childhood in front of everyone is difficult, but my brothers lived that life with me. We all went through it. We all remembered it. We'll never forget it no matter how hard we may try.

"No one in the community helped us. The police did nothing to stop my father from beating us. Broken bones, bruises. Nothing was enough for them to arrest my father for abuse. All we had was one another. We protected one another when no one else would. As we got older, Ian started to not feel well. The day our father died, Ian was having problems. Our father beat on him, calling him every name in the book. He hit me too that day. I'm pretty sure he raised a hand to all of us in a drunken rage, but my memory is a bit foggy since I was busy nursing my wounds."

I stop again, taking a few seconds to pull in some deep breaths. I can do this. I can get through this. I don't have a choice if I have any hope for Ian's future. "When my father raised a closed fist to my brother Finn, Ian had had enough, finding the closest thing next to him, and he hit my father over the head to stop him. Ian's never been a violent person. He's the nicest one of my brothers. He's the kindest soul even with everything he's been through. He only wanted my father to stop, and we all knew that when he was drunk, that wouldn't happen until he passed out. It was an accident and nothing more. Ian did what he needed to in order to protect us and himself. He did something no one else would do, not even the people who vowed to serve and protect us because they knew my father and thought of him as a friend. It didn't help that people in the community felt bad for my father since my mother left him with so many young kids. None of us deserved the life we were given. None of us deserved to be forgotten or beaten... especially not my brother Ian. When my father died, I confessed to the crime, wanting to make sure Ian got a chance to live without pain. Giving up a sliver of my life so my brother could know joy was worth it to me. We've been through enough since the day we were born. We deserve happiness. We deserve to be a family. We deserve to know what life is like without the threat of hurt just for existing. I ask you today to have mercy on my brother. For his sake and ours. Thank you." I take a step back as I fold my statement, locking eyes one more time with Ian.

His eyes are glassy, making it almost impossible for me not to get choked up. But when I turn around, Luna has her hand over her mouth, and tears are streaming down her face. She doesn't meet my gaze as I stalk back to my seat next to her.

I don't talk to her. I can't. If I do, I'll lose the little bit of control I have over my emotions. I keep my eyes straight ahead, blocking out my brothers as they each take a turn giving their statement and begging the judge to go easy on Ian.

When I start to become overwhelmed, Luna slides her hand to my lap and takes my hand, squeezing it. She doesn't say anything. She doesn't need to speak to me in order for me to understand all the things she wants to convey. I squeeze her hand back, having so much to say to her, but not having the ability to voice it.

"Mr. Walsh," the judge says once we've all had our say. "Please rise for sentencing."

My heart is pounding, and my palms are sweaty just like they were ten years ago when I was in his position. The overwhelming feeling of my stomach twisting and threatening to spill out onto the already stained carpet is stronger than it was when I was sentenced, but somehow, I keep everything down.

"Taking a life is a serious crime even when the act isn't premeditated. You've had years to live when the victim didn't get the same."

I growl, hating that he calls my father a victim.

He was the abuser. We were the victims.

He was the predator. We were the prey.

"Your brother served time for a crime he didn't commit. You allowed that to happen."

Here we go. His words aren't giving me hope for a light sentence.

"But the justice system did fail you and your brothers. You should've been protected. Having to take matters into your own hands should've never needed to happen. I am required by law to sentence you to time in jail. There is no probation option. Because of this, I'm sentencing you to three years in state prison with the possibility of parole after seventeen months."

I close my eyes, hating that Ian's going to serve seventeen months. It doesn't seem like much, but each day behind bars feels like an eternity. Time moves painfully slowly, and each day is a struggle to survive— both physically and mentally.

Ian turns around, glancing at each of us as if he's trying to memorize our faces. And he is. I know I did. I knew the moment had to sustain me for a long time and keep me going until the day I was given my freedom again.

The guard walks toward Ian, cuffs in hand, ready to haul him away. Luna hooks her arm around mine, plastering her body against me as she begins to cry.

"He'll be okay," I lie to her, rubbing the bare skin of her arm.

"He'll be okay," I lie to comfort her. "He'll be out in seventeen months. It'll go by fast."

She curls into me but keeps her eyes on Ian as they put the cuffs on him and lead him toward the same door he walked into the courtroom through. We all watch in stunned silence as the guard walks Ian out, fully expecting Ian to turn around one last time, but he doesn't.

"Damn," Luna whispers. "This is awful."

"He doesn't deserve this," Dylan says.

I stand there in stunned silence, staring at the door, wishing Ian would come back out and this would all be some cruel joke. But I know it's not possible. I know it'll never happen, no matter how badly I wish for it to be true.

"He'll be out in seventeen," Callum says to Finn. "At least the judge didn't make an example out of him."

"Yeah, man. I'm surprised he wasn't a bigger dick. They usually are."

"It's done," Finn says, ticking his head toward the entrance to the courtroom. "We should go. No use in staying here longer than we have to."

"Do you think we'll get to see him soon?" Luna asks me before we have a chance to move.

"It'll be a while. He'll let us know when he's able to have visitors, and he'll have to get us on the list and wait for us to be approved."

"This is bullshit," she mutters, finally releasing her hold on me, but not giving up the grip she has on my hand.

"Come back to our house. We have food," Rosie says. "I think we need to spend the day together as a family."

"You're coming, right?" Luna asks, peering up at me with so much hope.

"I can't. Got shit to do," I tell her.

She frowns as she lets go of my hand. "That's too bad, but I understand."

I hate that I'm adding more sadness to her eyes, but I need to be alone. My emotions are too all over the place, and I need to be by myself. I've never processed shit well around others, and today's no different.

"You're not coming?" Dylan asks me.

I shake my head. "I'll come another day."

His eyes narrow for a moment. "Sure," he mutters, knowing I'm lying.

"I need some time alone."

Luna touches my forearm. "Call me if you need to talk," she says so damn sweetly.

"I will. Thanks, Luna."

"I'm here for you, Nevin." She gives me a sad smile. "Whatever you need."

I lift her hand to my lips, kissing her fingers softly. "I can see why Ian cares for you so much."

If I didn't think he loved her or that she loved him, I'd maybe allow myself to dream that we could have a closer relationship than we do or ever will.

The one thing I won't do is step into his life and be a fill-in for him while he's absent. I'm not about to be a replacement for my brother.

His life is his.

I need to figure out what mine is about to become, and none of my plans involves falling for Luna Gallo.

4

LUNA

"LUNA, IT'S KAREN."

I stare at my phone screen, trying to make out the time. It's late. So late, I've already been asleep for hours.

"I don't know what else to do. I didn't know who else to call. I'm sorry it's so late."

"What's wrong?" I ask because Karen's never called me, and we barely know each other.

I can't imagine what she's calling me about. We're barely acquaintances and definitely not friends.

"Ian's brother is here." She sighs.

"Which one?"

"The one who just got out of jail."

"Okay," I yawn, covering my mouth with my hand.

"He's pretty damn drunk, and we're closing soon. He's alone, and I'm worried about him getting home. If he weren't Ian's brother…"

I pull myself up, fighting through another yawn. "I know. I know. You need me to get him?"

"Please, girl. I don't know who else to call, and I don't want to turn him outside."

I stretch before swinging my legs over the side. "I'll be there in twenty," I tell her.

"Thank you," she says, sounding relieved. "Catch you then."

I don't bother changing out of my leggings and tank top before I slip on a pair of flip-flops and head out the door. The air is crisp, a sure sign that fall is getting closer. But no matter how cool it becomes, I never put away my sandals.

Less than fifteen minutes later, I'm standing outside the bar I've spent more than a few nights at while Ian worked. The place is a step above a dive bar, but nowhere near swanky. Many nights, there were only a couple of regulars, especially outside of tourist and snowbird season, which gave us plenty of time to talk and laugh.

"Be strong and stern," I tell myself as I stand near the entrance. I take a few cleansing breaths and lift my chin before stalking through the door.

As soon as I'm inside, Karen catches my eye, dipping her chin toward Nevin. I give her a nod and mouth, "I've got him."

Nevin's back is to me as he sits on a stool, slumped over and sliding around an empty glass with one hand.

"Come on, Kar. One more. Pretty, pretty please," he begs her, using a soft, sweet voice.

"It was last call a half hour ago," she tells him, continuing to clean behind the bar. "Sorry, bud."

"Damn," he mutters and starts to climb to his feet. He leans against the edge, trying to stick his hand into his pocket, but he struggles. "I probably shouldn't have had the last one." His words aren't completely slurred, but the statement comes out slower than his normal cadence.

I slide onto the stool next to him, wanting to help, but not knowing what kind of drunk Nevin is. I've known all sorts, and not all of them are kind. "Hey," I say softly, ignoring his struggle with his pocket.

Nevin's head comes up, his dark-green eyes drinking me in. He stares at me for a few seconds, maybe trying to focus and seeing more than one of me. "Luna?" he whispers.

"Whatcha doing?" I ask, keeping things light.

A smirk slides across his face, and he sways backward until gravity puts him back on his stool. "Drinking."

"I can see that," I tell him, unable to cover my smile.

He's obviously going through some shit, but he seems lighter than he was earlier in the day. Getting drunk crossed my mind tonight, but I didn't feel like having a hangover tomorrow. Obviously, he didn't give two shits about the repercussions.

"You want a drink?" he asks me, forgetting what Karen said moments ago.

I shake my head. "I'm good."

"Well, I want another one." He raises a hand, trying to get Karen's attention, but she ignores him.

"I have booze at my place," I offer.

He lifts his hand toward his hair, brushing his fingertips through the short dark-brown strands. "The hard stuff?"

"Beer."

He scrunches his nose. "That's not booze, Lu."

"What is it?"

"Piss water."

I snort. "It'll get you drunk just the same."

He shakes his head. "Not true unless beer has changed that much since I went inside. Has it changed?"

"No. It's the same."

"Nothing else is," he says. "Everything is different."

"Not everything. I'm sure some things are the same, Nev."

He sighs. "More has changed than stayed the same. I feel like I've gone into an alien world and have to learn everything again."

"What's different?" I ask, trying to stay away from the topic of Ian.

"Cell phones." He pulls his from his pocket and sets it on the bar top between us. "I can't figure out what everything does."

"I can teach you."

He pushes it my way. "Put your number in and show me how to make a call or text you."

"Please."

"Please," he grumbles.

"If I show you, will you let me give you a ride home?"

He stares at me and doesn't answer right away. "I don't have a home," he says before looking away.

My heart sinks as his body language changes. "But you do, Nevin. It's still your home."

He fidgets on his stool and turns back toward me. "That place is nothing but a bad memory."

"Then come to my place," I say, not knowing what else to do, but understanding why Nevin wouldn't want to go back to the place where he grew up.

His eyes widen before the sloppy smirk slides back into place. "You want me to come over?" he waggles his eyebrows.

I nod. "Sure. We could have a sleepover."

"Can we make a fort?"

I stop myself from laughing. He looks so childlike and hopeful. "Of course. What's a sleepover without a fort?"

He shrugs. "Wouldn't know. Never had one."

"A fort or a sleepover?"

"Both," he mutters with a frown.

I haven't put much thought into their childhood and the absolute shittiness of the entire thing. So many things I did as a kid, I took for granted, figuring everybody had the same experiences. I couldn't have been more wrong.

Ian didn't talk to me too much about his childhood, wanting to stay in the present day. I knew why, but I never fully grasped the severity. I thought maybe they had a few normal days, but damn, I was completely wrong.

I place my hand gently on his shoulder. "Well, you're getting both tonight, bud."

His entire demeanor shifts. "Really?"

I grab his phone, typing my number into it before saving it. "For sure. We'll have a cell phone lesson too."

He pushes off the stool, coming to his feet. "Popcorn?"

"I have a bag," I tell him, climbing to my feet.

"I haven't had popcorn in so long."

My emotions are just as all over the place as his are. I can't imagine going without basic things for so long. I don't know a person who doesn't take a bag of popcorn for granted. I assume it'll always be there, but that's not the case for so many people going through some shit.

"I'm not even talking about prison. It wasn't some-thing we had as kids. Had to go to the dollar movies to get some." He takes a step and sways, but I quickly move to his side and grab his arm.

"Easy does it, big guy."

He gives me another sloppy smile as his eyes roam my face. "You're cute."

"You're drunk."

He chuckles, sounding lighter. "I am that, but you're still cute."

"I prefer pretty or hot as fuck, but cute will do."

He sways as I move his arm to my shoulder, letting him lean on me. "You're all of that too. Primo piece of ass."

"Don't hold back," I laugh, making eye contact with Karen, who looks more than relieved.

"I wasn't," he says playfully, taking his steps very slowly. "My brother should've locked you down."

I pull my head back, peering up at him. "Locked me down?" I keep him talking as we slowly walk toward the door. As long as he's concentrating on me, he's not thinking about leaving the place or another drink.

"A sweet, pretty thing like you is rare. That much hasn't changed. But the dumbass that he is, he didn't make you his, Lu. He should've made you his. Should've locked you up," he repeats.

"Can't cage a wild thing," I tell him, liking this side of Nevin over the grumpy human I've encountered the last few days.

He grazes his fingertips along the tender skin above my bicep. "You or Ian?"

"Both," I say, unable to hold back my laughter. "Your brother wasn't about settling down, and I was never interested in him in that way."

"And you?" he asks as soon as we're outside.

I stop walking to grab my keys. "Me what?"

He sways but catches himself, finding his balance. "Were you interested in settling down?"

"Not with Ian."

"That's not a yes."

"It's not a no, but it would have to be with the right one. I refuse to settle for mediocre."

"Life's too short for mediocre."

"You know it," I mumble, moving his heavy body toward the car when he struggles to walk straight. "Come on, Nev. Let's get you home and tucked in."

"Are you tucking me into your bed?"

"You can sleep in the spare bedroom," I tell him, making sure he knows nothing's going to happen. "Ro's old room."

"Fair enough," he whispers, but he doesn't stop moving. "But I don't do lace."

"No lace."

"Or silk."

"No silk either."

"Or flannel."

I stop walking and stare at him. "What do you do?"

"Cotton," he slurs.

"I figured you were a jersey guy," I tell him as I open the car door for him.

He grabs the doorframe, using it to hold his weight instead of me. "A what?"

"Jersey."

He blinks, looking so confused. "What the hell is jersey?"

"It's T-shirt material. The sheets are soft."

"They make sheets out of T-shirts?"

I laugh. "Not exactly, but it's the same material."

"I want those," he tells me, folding his body into my truck without smacking his head. "I want jersey."

"Well, lucky for you, big guy, those are the only sheets I have."

"No pink."

I roll my eyes. He's pretty damn demanding for a drunk guy who was lying in a jail cell not that long ago. "Sheets are white."

He relaxes into the seat, letting the back of his head touch the headrest. "Perfect."

I shut the door, cursing Ian as I round the front of my truck, ready for a ride home that's filled with questions about stupid things. At least Nevin's not belligerent. He could be a mean drunk. So many people are, and I've never dealt with them very well. Nevin's calmer... almost a different person. He's no longer the grumpy asshole, but a more zen and bougie version of himself.

Thankfully, Nevin keeps his eyes closed and his mouth shut during the short trip back to my place. He doesn't need my assistance walking to the front door of my apartment, but he doesn't push me away when I offer him the help.

"You're sweet."

"Thanks."

"And cute."

"You've told me this."

"Can never say it too much."

I'm starting to wonder if someone snatched his soul, putting a kinder and gentler being inside Nevin Walsh. He's turning into a giant cinnamon roll when I thought he was closer to a pit bull.

We barely make it into the living room when he falls sideways and lands right on the couch. He stretches out, his legs open, looking more like a wet noodle than a grown man.

"Leave me here," he says softly, throwing his arm over his face.

"No jersey?"

"No," he whispers behind his arm. "Right here is perfect."

I bend down, wanting to remove his boots so he doesn't dirty my area rug. He doesn't fight me as I grab his foot and start working the laces.

"Why are you so nice to me?"

I glance up, catching his green eyes peering down at me. "Why wouldn't I be?"

He shrugs. "No one's nice for no reason."

I frown. "Plenty of people are nice for no reason."

"My own father wasn't even nice."

He's getting heavy. His emotions are getting deeper in the silence of my apartment.

"You deserved better."

He blows out a long breath. "I don't know about that. Maybe I was paying penance for something."

"Like what?" I ask, slipping his first boot off, happy his socks are clean and he's not a smelly guy.

He scrubs a hand down his face. "Fuck if I know."

I make quicker work of the second boot, setting them next to the couch. "How many blankets do you want?"

"One."

"Pillow?"

"One."

I stalk away from him, kicking off my flip-flops as I walk, feeling the exhaustion taking over. I grab one pillow and one blanket from the closet in the hallway, fully expecting to find Nevin passed out by the time I get back.

But to my surprise, he's awake and sitting up.

"What's wrong?" I ask, tossing the pillow on the couch.

"I know you're only being nice to me because of Ian, but I'm okay with it."

I unfold the blanket, placing it on him. "That's not true, Nevin."

He grabs my hand before I have a chance to move away. "It is, and it's okay. I still appreciate you doing this and taking care of me. Doesn't matter why."

I curl my fingers around his and squeeze. "It's not because of Ian," I lie.

If Ian were still around, I'm pretty damn sure Nevin wouldn't have his ass on my couch. But that doesn't mean I wouldn't be nice to Nevin, and if he were in trouble, I'd still help. Ian and Dylan have become like family, and by extension, so have their brothers.

He releases my hand, lying back. "I'll make it up to you," he says, adjusting his body. "I promise."

"Just get some sleep."

He yawns. "Not hard on something so soft."

"Night."

"I'm sorry I'm drunk," he tells me with the softest, sleepiest voice. "I'm not usually like this."

"It's okay," I say, not wanting to tell him that I like this softer side of him better. "Sweet dreams."

"Night, Luna," he says as I switch off the light and head toward my bedroom, ready to pass out. "Sweet dreams, beautiful."

I smile to myself, wondering what the real Nevin Walsh is really like. I'm sure he's not even sure, but he'll eventually figure it out, and so will I. But for now, I'll do my best to be there when he needs me since I know Ian would want me to because best friends are there for each other no matter what. But I have a feeling it won't be that easy...nothing ever is.

5

LUNA

TWO WEEKS LATER

"GOD, LIFE SUCKS WITHOUT IAN AROUND." I SIT ON ONE side of the island in Rosie's kitchen with my head propped up on my palm, elbow bent and digging into the unforgiving granite counter. "Everything is just a little less..." I sigh and close my eyes for a moment, picturing Ian's smile.

Rosie places her knife next to the cutting board but keeps a hand on the onion. "He'll be back. Life won't be the same for a while, but time will go fast, and it'll be like it never happened."

"For us, it'll go fast, but not for him." I whisper the last part, watching Rosie as she goes back to chopping her onion and hopefully not her fingers.

I can't imagine how slowly each second must go by when sitting behind bars without any communication with the outside world. I don't think I'd survive that kind of existence for a day, let alone months.

"How's Dylan doing with it all?" I ask, trying not to think about the solitude of prison.

Her shoulders sag forward as she exhales. "He's been in a shit mood. It's taken a toll on him, but I can understand. If I had to live without you, even for a year, I don't know what I'd do."

"Hopefully we never have to find out."

She stares at me, waving the knife over the cutting board like she's a cooking professional. "Someone's going to go first, Einstein. We're not going to live forever."

I've never thought much about death, but thanks to my sister, I'm smacked in the face with our future reality. It sucks. All of it sucks. I haven't lived a day of my life without my sisters.

I lean back, tapping my fingernails on the granite, and come up with the craziest scenario possible. "Maybe we'll die together in a plane crash on our way to some exotic location when we're really old and can barely walk."

She blinks, looking at me like I'm nuts, which I very well may be at this point. The last few weeks have taken a toll on my sanity. "You're not right in the head, sis."

I nod slowly as I lift a glass of white wine to my lips, knowing I'm not playing with a full deck all the time. "Never claimed to be, but neither are you, babe."

"I'm normal," she argues, and I snort out a laugh, earning myself an icy glare. "I'm the most normal out of the three of us."

"That doesn't mean you're normal by any means. You do better at hiding your crazy."

"Normal is overrated," she says, lifting her knife again and going back to cutting the onions into perfect little pieces.

"Sure is." I watch her as she chops painfully slowly.

We're all shit cooks, a gene we clearly did not inherit. Even cutting vegetables is problematic, much to my grandmother's dismay. I wish I had the patience or the ability to chop up shit, but I can barely heat a package of ramen without fucking it up.

Rosie isn't much better, but the only thing she's good at is salsa and guacamole, and tonight, she's making a big batch of both.

"I was thinking…"

"About?" she asks without stopping, keeping her head down so she doesn't lop off a fingertip.

"I should drop by Nevin's. See if he needs anything."

That statement makes her stop dead in her tracks. Her head snaps up, eyes landing right on me. "Why?"

I shrug. "I'm sure he could use a friend. It can't be easy for him."

"He has his brothers."

I roll my eyes. "I have you too, but sometimes people need more than their own family. He's surrounded by men, and maybe he could use a woman around too to teach him things."

Her eyebrows rise, and I know what she's thinking without her saying the words.

"Not like that."

"Mmm-hmm."

"I promised Ian I'd look out for him."

"And how's that going for you?"

"He's totally blown me off. I've called a few times. Left him a couple messages and texts, but he hasn't texted back or called me...yet."

I haven't seen him since I picked him up at the bar. By the time I woke up in the morning, he was long gone. No note. No message. Nothing. It was as if he was never there.

"I think his silence is speaking loud and clear."

"The Walsh family isn't known for their communication, Ro. Dylan's the most talkative, and the man is practically a mute."

She tries to hide her laughter because she knows I'm right but hates to admit it.

"He can't ignore me forever," I tell her. I won't let him. If he's anything like his brothers, he'll sulk in his misery, wasting his freedom.

"The little I know of Nevin, I don't think your statement is true, Lu."

"You know I'm tenacious. Is he still living with his brothers?"

"That's one word for you," she mutters. She shakes her head, moving on to the few almost overly ripe avocados sitting in a basket in front of her. "He found a small efficiency in town at the place on the corner near the new bookstore a few blocks from the shop."

I wrinkle my nose. "The Wayward Traveler?"

So gross.

"Yep. That's it," she says.

"It's a total shithole."

And when I say shit hole, I mean shit hole. I rarely see a car stay very long in the parking lot, and the customers that do hang around tend to pay by the hour instead of the month or night.

She twists the avocado apart as I watch. "Nevin told everyone he wanted some time alone after spending years without any privacy. I'm pretty sure he would've lived in a cardboard box if it meant he could do it by himself."

"A cardboard box would be an upgrade from the Wayward."

"That ain't no lie, but a guy like him doesn't seem to care much about anything other than having a quiet place to lay his head."

"It can't be quiet there," I tell her, fingering the stem of my wineglass, trying to picture what the inside of a room at the Wayward Traveler must look like.

"I'm sure it's quieter than prison, and if it isn't, at least the noises are a whole lot different."

We both giggle, knowing exactly what happens there, even if no one talks about it.

"Maybe I'll bring him a plant to brighten the place up a little."

She snorts. "I'm sure that's exactly what he needs to make the place feel more like home."

I throw a stray piece of onion at her head. "What should I bring him, then, smarty-pants?"

"Nothing. Leave the man be for a while. Just give Nevin a little breathing room. He'll come around when he's ready."

I sigh, leaning against the back of the chair. "I'm not the most patient person."

"Toddlers are more patient." She chuckles this time, smiling up at me in between slices into the avocado.

Dylan stalks through the front door, toeing off his boots before he breezes into the kitchen. He grunts at me, which is his way of saying hello, before kissing Rosie on the cheek. "Smells good," he tells her.

"Me or the food?" she asks, staring him straight in the eye.

"Both," he whispers as he kisses her cheek.

"Ick." I pretend to gag at their cutesy talk.

They glance at me, but only Rosie speaks. "Button it up," she orders.

"Whatever," I groan.

"Where's the baby?" he asks her.

"Sal's sleeping. He had a long day of eating and shitting."

"He's a gold medalist at those." Dylan sighs. "I need

a beer." He moves toward the fridge and grabs a cold one from inside. "Anyone else?"

"Nope. We're good. I hope you're hungry. I'm making a lot tonight," Rosie tells her husband as she goes back to finishing the guac.

He nuzzles her neck but stays clear of her knife. "I'm starving, but babe, we can't only eat salsa and guac for dinner. A man needs more than that to survive."

"I picked up some enchiladas from the place you love, so we can reheat them to go with the chips, salsa, and guac. I know my man needs more to live."

He moves back to her side, staring at her profile. "You're the best."

"I know," she replies, smiling.

Only my sister can get away with picking up takeout and be praised for being the most amazing thing since sliced bread. The Walsh men aren't hard to impress, especially since they grew up on boxed generic mac and cheese and the cheapest frozen meals possible.

Dylan leans a hip against the counter, staying next to Rosie as he takes a swig of beer. I watch him as he downs half the bottle in a few quick gulps.

"Seen your brother lately?" I ask my brother-in-law.

He wipes his lips with the back of his hand and leans over the island. "Got to be more specific, Lu."

"Have you seen Nevin?" I ask again, being more specific as he requested, but he knew damn well which one I was talking about.

"Nope," he clips.

"Talk to him?"

"Yep."

"What did he say?" I ask.

Dylan stares at me for a full ten seconds without answering before he finally asks, "What's it matter?"

"She promised Ian she'd look after Nevin," Rosie explains before I can reply.

Dylan lets out a low rumble. "Look after him? He's grown the last time I checked and doesn't need a babysitter."

I give Dylan the middle finger. "No shit. I don't plan on babysitting him. I just want him to know he has people."

"He knows he has people," Dylan tells me.

"People besides you and his other brothers."

Dylan shakes his head as he moves the beer bottle back toward his mouth. "He's fine, Lu. He's a big boy. If he isn't, he'll figure it out."

"I'm sure he could use another friend."

"I think he had enough of those the last decade."

I purse my lips and bite down the shitty words that are dying to come off my tongue. "Maybe I'll drop by and see him tonight. Maybe bring him some salsa and guac if Rosie can spare a little extra. Invite him to go shopping or something with me tomorrow."

"I'm sure that'll go over big," Dylan says sarcastically. "Every man's dream is to go shopping with a woman."

Rosie elbows him hard enough that he lets out a

loud *humph*. "You can take as much as you want and whatever you want, but I'm telling you right now, the man wants to be alone."

"Thanks, Ro. I'm sure he'll love a homemade snack," I say, ignoring their unsolicited advice.

"Not the enchiladas, though," Dylan adds, pointing to the boxes of takeout. "Those are staying here."

"Whatever," I grumble as I raise the wine to my lips to polish off the small amount left in my glass. "Their enchiladas are only okay. You can keep them."

"Wasn't giving them up," he replies.

"You never answered my question," I say to Dylan.

"Which was?"

I let out an exasperated sigh. "What did Nevin have to say? Is he okay?"

"He's fine. He has a roof over his head and a bed to sleep in. There's nothing else the man wants."

"A woman..." Rosie giggles. "Ten years is a long time without one."

"Pretty sure there're plenty of those around his place too," Dylan says with a salacious smile.

"He deserves better than a prostitute," I sneer.

"Nevin never had trouble with the ladies, Lu. I'm sure he isn't going for dirty pussy when he can pretty much have his pick," Dylan says, as if he's talking about picking out fruit at the grocery store and not sex.

"You're an asshole," I mumble.

"What'd I say that wasn't true?"

I slide off the stool, pissed off for some strange

reason, and head to the cabinet, pulling out two containers. "Nothing," I snap.

"Lu, what's wrong?" Rosie asks.

I set the plastic bowls on the counter next to her, tapping my foot. "Nothing."

"Uh, yeah. That ain't going to fly. I know you better than anyone else, and I know when you're pissed. And you're pissed."

"I'm not."

She stops mashing the guac as she stares at me. "Want to try that again? You got a thing for Nevin?"

I shake my head. "I don't know the guy, Ro. How am I supposed to have a thing for him?"

She shrugs. "Fuck if I know, but you don't usually get so upset about something so stupid."

I lean over, rubbing one side of my head. "I don't know why I'm so upset about it. He's not my man. I just feel like he deserves more...something better after everything he gave up for Ian."

"He does deserve better, and right now, the man wants a little time to himself and some peace and quiet."

"I can be quiet."

Dylan scratches his beard, staring at me like I'm crazy too. Something he and my sister have in common. "Whatever you want to do, Lu. Just know he's not going to be overly excited to have uninvited company."

"Who said I'm staying?" I push the containers toward my sister, wanting her to fill them so I can get out of there. "I'm just going to drop off some food and run. Everybody has to eat."

"So, you aren't going to stay and talk?" Dylan asks.

"No." I don't even convince myself with that one-word answer.

"Maybe Nevin would like company tonight, baby. You never know. Your brother's not the same person you knew when you were younger."

"I left so long ago, and he was so young. I don't know who he really was then, and I certainly don't know who he is now. Watch yourself, Lu. Just because he once did something honorable doesn't mean he's a nice guy now. Don't go over there with any grand illusion that you two are going to become best friends like you did with Ian."

I cross my arms, glaring at Dylan even though his words are coming from a good place. "I have no grand delusions or illusions that Nevin and I will be friends, let alone best friends. I'm being nice."

"As long as we're on the same page about expectations," Dylan says, pulling on his beer with his smug lips.

I take the spoon from Rosie and fill the two containers like I'm in a competition that's based more on speed than accuracy.

She watches in stunned silence as guac and salsa go flying. She's seen every mood I have, and she knows when it's best not to engage. And she's not engaging.

"I'm not an idiot, Dylan. I'm sorry you never had

many people be nice to you in your life, but this is what my people do."

"Be careful. Call me later," my sister says before I have a chance to make an exit.

"Love you," I tell her.

"Love you too," she says back.

"Love you too, Lu," Dylan says to me.

And even though I'm annoyed and unusually cranky, I still say to him, "Love you too, asshole."

I stopped by Nevin's motel room on the way home from Rosie's, but no one answered. I sat in the parking lot, watching the people come and go for a half hour before I gave up and headed home.

I am about to drop my phone onto the bed, but something stops me. I press on Nevin's name and call him. Six rings and nothing except the basic voice mail greeting. He hasn't bothered setting up a personal one yet. And from the little I know about Nevin, I doubt he ever will.

When there's a long beep, I start talking, "Hi, Nevin. It's Luna again. Just wanted to check on you and invite you to my grandparents' for dinner tomorrow. It's totally casual, but there's tons of homemade food. I'll try texting you in—"

There's another beep. "Fucker," I hiss, hating how short the messages need to be.

I don't bother calling again. I head straight to my text messages and send off a few, hoping he'll reply. I know Dylan's right about shopping, so I try a different tactic. They say the way to a man's heart is through his stomach, so I try that route first.

Me: Hey, Nev. Want to hang out tomorrow? Maybe grab some things you need?

I stare at the screen, waiting to see the three dots, showing that he is replying, but I see nothing.

Me: I'll pick you up at one. I'm off.

Me: No pressure.

Before I have a chance to shoot off another text, the family chat starts blowing up my phone.

Stone: When is it too early to bring a girl I'm seeing?

Tamara: Are you seeing her or sleeping with her?

Stone: Technically?

Tamara: Yes, dumbass.

Carmello: If you bring a girl you're bangin' to dinner, she'll think she's more important than she is. Are you really serious about her, Stone?

Stone: Nah, man. She's not long-term material, but she could suck the chrome off a bumper.

Lily: Nice, little brother. I thought you were a gentleman.

Stone: Sis, I know when to behave and when to unleash the beast.

Trace: Beast mode has been officially activated.

Tamara: Are you three morons out at the clubs?

Asher: Fuck yeah. You should all be here.

Gigi: Too old. Kids kill all fun.

Jett: Ain't that shit the truth.

Rocco: They aren't that bad. Put the kids to bed and get busy making another.

Tamara: No freaking way. You have more. I'm done. Pussy closed.

Mammoth: Princess, don't lie.

Tamara: No more babies, Josiah.

I giggle because I can never think of Mammoth as Josiah. Nothing about him goes with the name. He's a Mammoth all the way. From his size to his attitude, he's larger-than-life and can make most men shit their pants with a single glance.

Trace: I thought the three of us made a pact. No bitches on Sunday until we're ready to settle down.

Asher: Yep.

Me: Classy. Way to leave out the only female cousin.

Stone: You want in, li'l cuz?

Me: I'm older than you, jagoff.

Stone: But you're still little. You barely come up to my shoulder. When you grow a foot, I'll rethink the nickname.

Rebel: Ah, to be young again...and dumb.

Rocco: Reb, you aren't old, baby. You're more beautiful than the day I met you.

Jo: We should all plan a night out. Show these young boys how it's really done.

Trace: Spare us the misery.

Pike: You three have no idea what fun really is. You're happy if some chick, any chick, rubs her body against your crotch.

Asher: Maybe that's what they did in the old days, Grandpa. Chicks are different now.

I roll my eyes. My younger cousins, all boys, are the biggest dipshits ever. Asher and Stone are in college, living the frat life, burying themselves in every skirt that comes their way. And there are a lot of them too. I visited them one weekend and vowed never to do that shit again. Frat life isn't for me, but they revel in it. They were born for that bullshit. Trace is older than them, but you'd never know it by his behavior.

Arlo: I'm going to bop the three of you when I see you tomorrow for the old comment and calling women bitches.

Asher: You got to catch us. Does your scooter move that fast?

Rosie: You're cruisin' for a bruisin'.

Trace: That's what the old people say.

Pike: Fuckers.

Trace: Later, bitches. We're following some chicks to another club. It's a negative on inviting her to dinner tomorrow, Stone.

Me: Do you even know these girls?

Stone: Again, the one gave me head. I know her well enough.

I shake my head, wondering how I'm straight with assholes like my cousins in my life.

Tamara: Were we that stupid at their age?

Gigi: I don't think so…

Lily: You were. I can attest to it.

Pike: Baby, you left a bar with me and barely knew my name.

Gigi: It was a bet.

Pike: You're not winning your case.

God, I love my family. I barely think about how lucky I am to have them in my life, but I know I didn't grow up like many of my friends. Not only is our family huge, but we love one another, and we've spent every weekend and sometimes more with one another.

On top of that, most of us either work at Mammoth and Tamara's auto repair, my uncles' investigation company, or our tattoo shop. We are up one another's asses constantly, and somehow, we make it work.

Carmello: Everyone's an idiot at some point in their life, especially when we're young.

Mammoth: Some of us more than others and for more years than we care to admit.

Tamara: Is that a dig at me, sweetie?

Mammoth: Absolutely not.

Tamara: Sure thing, sparky. I don't believe you.

I close the family chat, leaving them to reminisce about the good old times. I almost forget about Nevin not replying, but I catch myself, opening my texts to him to be sure.

Still nothing.

Jerk.

It doesn't matter.

I can't sit here all night, wondering if he's okay.

There's only one thing to do, and no one can stop me. I'm going to go to the Wayward Traveler and camp out in my car until Nevin lets me inside.

6

NEVIN

I UNWRAP THE CANDY BAR I SNAGGED FROM THE vending machine as I walk back to my room, paying no attention to the people in the parking lot.

"Hey, Daddy," a woman calls out, wearing a cropped tank top and a skirt that leaves very little to the imagination. "I can be your fantasy!" she yells louder when I ignore her. "I can do things to you that you never imagined."

While the thought of sinking into a woman sounds great, her pussy won't be the first one I've had in ten years…not even if there was a gun to my head.

As soon as I'm back inside my room, I kick off my boots and collapse into the chair, throwing the bag of chips I bought on the table. This is tonight's dinner. But no matter what, at least it's a meal I chose, and it wasn't prepared by inmates.

When I dreamed of getting out of prison, this isn't the way I imagined it. "What fucking bullshit," I mutter to no one except myself. "Total bullshit."

When that night happened and the cops showed up, I offered myself up on a silver platter. There was no way in hell I'd let Ian sit behind bars where he, once again, would be treated like shit and continue to get sicker. I knew his only option of getting any help would be if I went to prison in his place.

None of us thought I'd get a ten-year sentence. How fucking ridiculous and corrupt of my small-town police department and prosecutor's office. They knew damn well why it happened. They knew for years that our father had mistreated us. But no one helped, and an entire town turned a blind eye to the abuse because it was easier on them.

Fuck the kids…fuck us.

If it weren't for my brothers still being here, I would've left town the second my feet hit the dirt on the outside. But they're all I have, and after being apart for so long, I have to stick around. I can't abandon them. Maybe after a few months, when no one seems to notice, I can slip away to some place where no one knows me or my history.

As I reach for the bag of chips, there's a knock at the door.

So help me God, if it's that hooker, I'm going to lose my mind.

"What?" I snap as I pull the door open without looking.

Standing right in front of me is Luna, holding two containers and a bag of tortilla chips in her arms. "Hi," she squeaks, eyes wide and round from the way I snapped at her. "I brought you some food."

Damn, she looks good. Her long blond hair cascades over her shoulder, covering some of her cleavage. Her red lipstick makes it impossible for me not to think every possible dirty thought too.

"Sorry," I mutter.

"I called and texted you a few times," she says cheerfully.

"I didn't get anything," I lie, knowing damn well I ignored every single message she sent my way. "My phone must be jacked, and I still don't have the hang of the thing. It's complicated."

She stares at me, studying my face, not knowing if I'm lying or not, which I am. "Maybe," she says, buying my bullshit. "It's okay." She leans over, looking into my room. "Can I come in?"

Fuck!

I don't want company.

"I'm expecting some friends," I lie again.

She raises her eyebrows. "Oh. Well…okay." She looks like I've punched a puppy, and the guilt gnaws at my insides.

My gaze drops to her hands, and my stomach rumbles,

reminding me a candy bar and small bag of chips aren't enough to sustain me. "But you can for a minute," I finally say when she doesn't offer me the shit she's holding.

Luna gives me an awkward smile, but she doesn't move until I step back, letting her inside.

She slinks past me, tits almost brushing against my chest, and goes straight to the table. "I'll just put these here," she says as she places the two plastic containers and the bag down gently. "Rosie made salsa and guac. They're the best and only thing she can cook. I figured you'd like something to munch on tonight."

"Thanks," I tell her as she leans over, arranging the containers and taking off the lids.

I stare at her from behind.

Her ass is sheer perfection. Hourglass figure and legs for fucking miles. If it weren't for this fucked-up situation, she's exactly the type of chick I'd have under me within minutes.

Luna turns toward me and misses the way I'm staring at her. Thank fuck. "Sure thing," she replies with so much cheer and sweetness, my teeth hurt.

She glances around, spinning in a circle, and takes in everything that the Wayward Traveler has to offer in their fine accommodations. "This is…" She pauses and does another pass, trying to come up with the right words.

Someone like her has probably never stepped foot in a place like this before tonight. From her fancy heels to her perfectly done hair, the bitch is too classy for a shit-hole like this.

"It's not too bad," she says slowly and lying through her perfectly straight white teeth.

"It'll do." I sit in the chair next to the food she brought, watching her as she starts to walk around the room as if she's looking for something. She runs her hand down the comforter and pulls back like the scratchy material burned her fingertips. "But this is awful."

"It's fine." I tear open the tortilla chips, keeping my eyes trained on her.

She shakes her head. "I was wondering if you wanted to go shopping."

"No," I bite out as I pop a chip into my mouth without the extras.

Her eyebrow rises again as she stares at me, blinking. "No?"

"No." I shake my head.

"Okay," she whispers.

"I have what I need."

She stares at me, confused. "You have what you need?"

"A few tees. Some jeans. Boots. I'm set."

"Maybe some new underwear?" she asks, looking so fucking hopeful.

A look I know I must extinguish and quickly.

"Don't wear them. Don't want them."

She swallows, and my words don't land quite the way I want them to.

"I don't shop."

"I can shop and bring them to you," she offers, being so fuckin' sweet again. Too sweet for a damaged, fucked-up guy like me.

"Nope."

She tilts her head like she heard me wrong. "No?"

"No, Luna. I don't need clothes. I don't need you to buy me anything either."

"I'm just trying to—"

"I don't need your help."

Damn. I'm a prick. The chick is trying to be nice, but it's best if I make it clear, we're not going to be BFFs. I'm not going to step into the shoes of my brother, filling the hole left by his absence.

She sits down on the bed but does it with grace, like she's trained for years how to sit instead of plop. "I promised Ian I'd check on you."

"You checked. Promise fulfilled."

She purses her lips. "You're not nice, Nevin."

"A decade in prison will do that to a person."

God, I'm such an asshole. She's so damn beautiful, and I know if I spend too much time with her, I'll ruin her. Ian made me promise to look out for her, but he didn't know what he asked or how much I'd changed since I went inside.

She hangs her head, fiddling with her fingertips,

unable to look at me. "I can't imagine what you went through."

"Hopefully you never will." I relax back into the chair, rubbing my palms down the old, worn-away stain of the wood handles. It's the only thing I can do to stop from launching myself across the room and kissing her sweet, beautiful face.

The plumpness in her lips grows fuller as she almost pouts on the same spot where I sleep. "Do you want to come to dinner at my grandma's tomorrow, then?"

"Negative."

"Dylan will be there." She tries again.

"Doesn't matter. I'll pass."

She tips her head up so I can see her entire face in the dim lighting of my room. "Are you always so difficult?"

I raise a shoulder. "I don't know what I am anymore."

"You want to talk about whatever is bothering you?"

"No."

"You sure?"

"Yep. I'm sure I don't want to talk," I say softly, hoping to lessen the blow that she'll no doubt feel.

She sighs, leaning back on the bed and placing her palms on the shitty comforter. The position makes her chest stick out more and pulls at the V neckline of her shirt, making her cleavage unmissable. "I was really hoping we could be friends."

"I don't have women as friends."

"Why not?" she asks, swinging a leg out in front of her, making her tits wobble.

"Because I don't want to fuck my friends."

She blinks. "You want to fuck me?" she whispers.

I stare at her with a straight face. "Ten years of not getting laid and I'll pretty much fuck anyone besides the dirty bitches in the parking lot."

Her face turns red, and while my answer didn't hit the spot she wanted, it got my point across. I do want to fuck her, but in no way am I allowing that shit to happen.

Yep. Total prick.

I'm not going to be anyone's pity bang. This chick so badly wants to help me, I have no doubt she'd spread her legs and give me her pussy because she thinks it will make me feel better.

"You're an asshole."

"Never said I wasn't."

She stands quickly and heads for the door. When her hand touches the handle, she turns to face me. "I'm not giving up on you yet, Nevin. You need a friend, and no matter what, it's going to be me."

"Good luck to you, babe."

"I'll wear you down. Just you wait and see," she says before marching out the door and slamming it behind her.

I grab my phone and immediately call Dylan. "What the fuck is up with Luna, man?"

Dylan laughs. "She stopped by?"

"You know she did. Am I her personal mission or some shit?"

"Yep."

"I don't need someone watching over me."

"Too fucking bad, man. She promised Ian she'd watch over you, and Luna usually follows through on shit."

"I don't need Ian's woman up my ass all the time. And I promised him I'd look after her."

"They aren't together like that, bro. I told you this. They are friends."

"I don't care what they are. I don't do seconds, especially his."

"Whoa. Whoa. Whoa. No one said you should do her. Actually, don't look at Luna that way. I like the girl, but you and she would be nothing except a disaster, and I don't feel like cleaning up the wreckage you'd no doubt leave."

"Maybe she'd hurt me? Ever think of that."

Dylan laughs. "Totally possible. Luna's sweet as sunshine when she likes you, but wicked as the devil too. She's vulnerable right now, and I don't want her to do something she'll regret later."

"She isn't the only one who's sad," I tell him, grinding my teeth together.

"I'm warning you, Nevin, you need to keep your hands off her and your dick out of her."

"Hands and dick went nowhere near her."

"Good."

But now that the asshole is making her off-limits…

"I mean it, Nevin. Don't fuck up my marriage because you want a piece of ass. The girl doesn't need to be ruined by you."

"How would I ruin her?"

"We're all fucked in the head, and there's no doubt in my mind some of your past will rub off on her in a way that won't be good for any of us."

"Our past," I correct him.

"I moved on. Got help. Found a good woman who makes me want to be a better man."

"Maybe I want that too, asshole. Ever think of that?"

"You can have it. Just not with Luna."

"Am I not good enough?"

Dylan grunts. "Never said that, but…"

"I'm not a criminal, fucker. I know it's hard for you to wrap your brain around that reality, but I didn't kill that bastard. I took the fall for my brother, *our brother*, which is more than I can say for you. I'm an innocent man who gave up ten fucking years to protect Ian. Did you do that?"

Dylan sighs on the other end of the phone. "I didn't."

"Then stop talking to me like I'm trash and not worthy of your wife's sister."

"Fuck around with whomever you want, Nevin, except Luna. I'm begging you. It won't end well for any of us."

"She ain't my type anyway," I tell him, trying to

alleviate some of his worry, although I don't owe him shit.

"Liar."

"I got to go."

"Nevin…"

"Bye," I tell him and hang up.

Fuck him and the perfect life he created.

Let him squirm a little.

7

LUNA

"YOU WANT A BLANKET?" ROSIE ASKS ME AS I CURL ON my side on the chaise lounge by the pool.

The sunshine feels great today. Not too hot for the first time in months. This is fall in Florida. There are no leaves to change colors, no crispness to the air.

"No. I'm comfy."

She stands over me, casting a shadow near my feet. "You sure?"

"Completely." I wave my hand, letting her know she's blocking the sun.

Rosie lies down on the chaise next to mine and lifts her arms upward, locking her fingers behind her head. "It's a pretty day," she says, beating around the bush.

She wants answers about last night but hasn't come right out and asked.

"Winter is right around the corner."

"So…" she says, drawing out the word.

"It went like shit," I tell her, answering her question before she asks, which could've taken more minutes than I have to give. "He was an asshole."

"Was he mean? Did he hurt your feelings?"

I raise myself up on one arm and stare at her. "Why would you think that?"

She lifts a shoulder, giving me a sorrowful smile. "I don't know. We don't know him, and I figured—"

"He didn't do anything to me. He's just not friendly."

"I'm sure prison can suck the friendly right out of a man." She glances up at the clouds, her eyes following the path of one across the sky. "I'm sure he's pissed at the world. Wouldn't you be?"

"Yeah, Ro. I'd be super pissed, but I was being nice to him, and he was being rude and difficult."

Rosie reaches over, touching the top of my hand. "You have to remember they didn't grow up like we did. Their kindness and social skills are different."

"Dylan isn't such an asshole."

"Dylan had years away from his family to figure out how to be nicer than the rest. That time for Nevin was spent being surrounded by criminals."

I sigh.

"Ian wouldn't want you to make yourself feel worse than you already do. If Nevin wants to be alone, you may have to let him be," she adds.

Asher, Stone, and Trace—our dumbass cousins—

come barreling out with their swimsuits on, carrying towels, and elbowing one another in a fit of laughter.

Rosie watches them as they throw down their towels on the chairs nearby. "What's so funny?" she asks them.

Stone, who's grown like a weed the last few years, stretches his arms, looking every bit like his father, my uncle Mike. "Just talking about the chicks we met last night."

"Where did you three end up?" I ask as they wade into the pool like they're refined instead of the punk boys they are.

"A hot club down in Tampa," Asher, Tamara's brother, answers before dipping his head under the water.

"It was fucking mint, but my parents can't know we ever went there," Trace adds.

"Aunt Izzy and Uncle James would be pissed," Stone tells Trace. "But honestly, what could they do, bro? We're in college. You've been out for a while. You don't even live at home anymore."

"I'm pretty sure Uncle James could find a way to make Trace pay." Stone laughs, spreading his arms out along the top of the pool as he takes up residence at a spot near the other side.

"It's more my mom I'm worried about," Trace says.

Even if he's not the brightest, at least he's smart enough to be worried about Aunt Izzy. She can make grown men cower.

"Aunt Izzy is scary as fuck, yo," Asher tells him,

looking back into my grandparents' house, where Izzy is helping my grandmother in the kitchen. "She's one person I wouldn't cross."

"Try having her as a mom. Your parents are cool, Ash. Mine…not so much."

"Why would they get pissed about a club? You three are always at clubs." Rosie looks at me, and I shrug.

"Makes no sense," I tell her.

"Well…" Trace winces. "It wasn't a dance club."

My eyes widen because I know what he's saying without him having said it. "You went to one of those clubs?" I ask, shocked at my three cousins and their boldness—or maybe it's more stupidity.

"Wasn't in the plans, but the girls wanted to go," Asher explains.

"Women," Stone adds, checking out his muscles as he flexes his biceps, and the water dotting his skin sparkles with his movement.

Men.

These three have the biggest heads. Cocky isn't even a strong enough adjective to describe them. They're emotional wrecking balls for the opposite sex, blowing through girls like they're disposable.

"We were drinking, just hanging out, and started talking with them. They asked if we'd take them to this other club, without telling us what kind of club it was." Asher shakes his head.

"Wait," I say, moving my body to sit up and face the boys. "You met three random chicks and they invited you to a sex club, and you just went…no questions asked?"

Trace stares at me with his eyebrows pulled downward. "Well, yeah, cousin. That's how it works."

"That's how it works?" I repeat, confused, because that's not how it works unless you're an idiot.

But then I remember they're walking balls of hormones. Driven by nothing more than their dicks and the need to feed their libido.

"When three chicks ask you to go somewhere, anywhere, you don't say no or ask questions," Stone explains like it's the written law of bro code. "You just go."

"Three hot chicks, at that. They could've asked us to go to a dark alley, and we would've gone," Asher continues to explain the stupidity like it is the way of the world, and somehow, I've missed the lesson.

"Stupid," Rosie mutters. "It's shocking you three are still alive with all the dumb shit you've done."

Trace shrugs. "It's hard to kill a Greek god."

I roll my eyes. "You three aren't Greek, and you're not gods either."

"I'm half Greek," Stone says, raising his hand in the air. "And based on my muscles, I'm as close to a god as a woman can come." He waggles his eyebrows, earning a groan from Rosie and me.

Asher nudges him in the ribs. "Your lips to God's ears, brother."

"Do the girls you hang out with like your attitude?"

Rosie asks them. "You three ooze confidence and not in the way that would catch my eye."

"Not trying to catch their eyes, Ro. Also, based on the way they cling to us like lint on a dark sweater, I'd say the chicks dig the attitude. They're like moths to a flame, babe."

I gag a little, pretending to vomit at their ridiculousness.

"You three are not all that," Ro tells them.

"The way our phones blow up would say otherwise," Asher tells her without so much as a smile.

"Women are dumb," I mutter.

"Yep," Rosie says to me with a nod.

"Did you end up at the same club your parents used to go to?" I ask Trace, knowing he'll hate being reminded that his parents once had a more adventurous sex life than he could ever imagine.

He instantly winces. "No, cuz. That would be fucking weird. We ended up at a different place on the other side of town. Thank fuck, too. The last thing I need is for them to find out we were there."

"Truth," Asher whispers as he walks through the water to the other side. "We'd get an earful."

"The community isn't that big," I remind them. "I'm sure they'll catch wind of it eventually."

I ignore them as they go on and on about the women and the club. All topics I don't want to hear my little cousins discussing. The less I know about their sex lives, the better.

There's only one thing on my mind, and it's getting Nevin to open up and find some happiness in his life.

Stone peers back at me, catching me off guard. "What's wrong? Something happen?"

"No," I answer quickly.

He doesn't stop staring, and I look away, hating when he tries to figure me out. "I'm not buying it. Your sparkle is gone, babe."

"Just thinking about Ian," I tell him, hoping it's enough to get him to back off with the line of questioning.

"Understandable, but there's something else," he pushes. "I know you too well."

"Whose ass do we need to kick?" Trace asks, making a fist and smashing it into his other palm.

"No one's."

I have no doubt they'd at least try. The men in this family, even the youngest ones, are protective to a fault. They'll rush into battle without having a game plan, and by sheer, dumbass luck, they somehow come out unscathed.

"She's trying to make friends with Nevin," Rosie blurts out, never able to keep her big mouth shut.

Trace sucks in air between his teeth. "Fuck. For real?"

Stone shakes his head. "Bad idea."

Asher bobs in the water, his eyes now trained on me. "The prison guy?"

"He's not a criminal," I tell them, feeling defensive about a man I barely know.

"But he was in prison for years," Asher explains, like I don't know the reality that was Nevin's life.

"He didn't do it. He didn't deserve to be there," I shoot back immediately. "He took the rap for his brother."

As if my three cousins sent out an invitation to the rest of the family, the entire crew marches out of the sliding glass doors.

"What's going on?" Gigi asks as she sits down at the edge of my chair, noticing the sudden quiet.

"Nevin took her sparkle," Asher says with a shrug, ratting me out like a traitor.

"He what?" Tamara asks her brother. "Her sparkle?"

"Fuck," Dylan hisses.

"We'll take care of him," Mammoth says, making the same motion Trace did a moment ago with his fist. "No one's going to be mean to Luna."

Why are all men cavemen? Not everything can be solved with a fist. And while, at times, it may be necessary, Nevin doesn't need an ass-whooping; he needs a goddamn hug.

"I'm not helpless, people. I can take care of myself, and Nevin didn't steal my sparkle—or anything else, for that matter."

"Did you sleep with him?" Gigi asks, making my body rock backward.

God, she can be such a judgmental bitch. Sure, I'm

not a virgin and have slept with my fair share of guys, but I'm not throwing my pussy around to every passerby.

"No, Gigi. That would require him to be nice and for me to be willing, which he isn't and I'm not."

"When do you need a guy to be nice for you to sleep with him?" Rosie asks with a small laugh. "If my memory serves me…"

Here we go. My sister has a memory like a built-in filing cabinet. She never forgets anything and pulls up bullshit from ten years ago like it happened yesterday.

I give her the middle finger. "I do have standards."

Gigi isn't fazed by my gesture when she keeps talking, "So, you're saying if he were nice, you'd sleep with him?"

"No," I bite out, keeping my middle fingers highly visible.

"Lies," Rosie teases. "He's your type."

"What's my type?" I ask her, sitting up now because I'm not going to take what feels like an attack lying down.

"Grumpy and gorgeous."

I wrinkle my nose. "I don't like grumpy guys, and he's not gorgeous."

"You do. Ian was the exception, although he had a grumpy side too sometimes," Gigi says. "And unless you're blind, Nevin is cute."

"You just haven't found the right amount of grumpy and gorgeous to keep your attention long enough.

You're a fixer, babe. You always want to help, and Nevin is the perfect match for a girl like you, but he isn't having it," Rosie explains.

"And he never will," Dylan adds. "Stay away from him, Lu. I already told you."

I narrow my eyes at Dylan, hating him just a little bit more. "That's your brother you're talking about."

"And you're now my sister-in-law. Both of you are family, and I'm telling you *again*, no matter what Ian asked, he wouldn't want you hurting because Nevin is an asshole. Steer wide and clear of him."

"He may be an asshole, but at least he's honorable," Jett says, sitting next to Lily at the table off to the right with his arm around her shoulders.

"Don't you start," Gigi tells him, pointing her finger his way. "Honorable or not, I don't want my sister with him."

"What do you even know about him?" Nick asks Gigi after her swift and definitive condemnation of Nevin.

Gigi waves her hand. "Don't need to know more than he's Dylan's brother, and while he did something honorable, he doesn't have much to offer my sister except misery. And based on the sad puppy dog look on her face, I'd say he's already giving her a heavy dose."

Carmello clears his throat, entering the fray. "You can't judge a man for being the way he is after serving time in prison for a crime he didn't even commit. Add to that, the fact that he did it to save his brother's life.

Sorry, Dylan, but that's a man I wouldn't mind my sister being with."

Dylan gives him a chin lift. "Lucky for you, you don't have a sister. And I know, at his core, my brother is a good man, but it's going to take him time to find out who he is, Luna. I just don't want you to become part of his healing process. I think he's going to leave a lot of damage in his wake. Walsh men don't do well with feelings, and you feel too much. You know?"

I cross my arms over my chest, hating that they're talking about my life and trying to decide everything for me. Add in the fact that they're judging Nevin before even giving him a chance, and I'm over the conversation. I climb to my feet, glancing around at all of them. "You all need to worry about your own lives. Not mine. I've got mine handled. Stop trying to read me and figure out what's wrong with me or who did something to upset me. Worry about yourselves and not me. Understood?" I tap my foot, waiting for their responses as they gawk at me in complete shock.

"Understood," Lily answers for the group. "We're just worried."

"Worry about someone else. Maybe worry about the three dumbasses who met some random bimbos last night and ended up at a sex club," I announce, dropping the bomb which will no doubt lead straight back to James and Izzy.

"Fuck, Lu. You had to out us like that?" Stone calls

out, smacking the water with his hand, sending a few drops in my direction.

"Shit," Trace mutters. "I can't believe she just did that."

I march off, leaving the boys with a lot of explaining to do, along with even more groveling.

I've never been a tattletale, but I needed a reprieve from all their eyes on me, trying to tell me what to do.

Whether or not I try again with Nevin is my business and no one else's.

8

NEVIN

"Hey," my brother says as soon as I open the door to my motel room. "We need to talk."

I don't move out of the doorway. We've said all that needs to be said. He hates me, and my feelings toward him aren't too far off. "I don't think we have much to say to each other."

He peers down, kicking the tip of his boot into the cement walkway. "*I* need to talk to you. You don't need to talk back, but I have shit I need to get off my chest."

"Sounds like it's your problem. How about this? I let you off the hook for whatever you have to say. You don't need to come in, talk through our past. What's done is done. Leave it all behind us."

"Please, Nevin," he begs. "Ian wouldn't want this for us."

"You're such a dick." I move to the side, letting him into my room.

He steps inside, looking around. "Interesting place," he mutters. "Not quite what I thought it would be like inside."

"It's better than prison."

He blinks slowly, shaking his head. "I'm sorry. I can't imagine—"

"No. You can't," I snap, stalking past him toward the bed. The mattress sags and squeaks under my weight as I sit. "You wanted to talk. So, talk."

He collapses into a chair across from me. "I should've stayed."

"Yep," I clip out. "No shit."

"I should've been the one to protect you guys from Dad. I fucked up. I should have fought for you guys, but I knew no court would've given me custody. I was in a shitty position, and the only thing I could think to do was leave. I thought if I left, Dad wouldn't be so angry, and maybe he wouldn't hit anyone anymore."

"He did hate you the most," I tell him, not caring how he feels. My father did too. He had pure hatred for Dylan, but it wasn't as if he loved any of us. He didn't even like us. "But way to go, thinking like Mom. How'd that work out for us?"

"I thought he'd mellow if I wasn't around, but you're right. I was stupid. I couldn't think clearly when I was there."

Mellow? My father was about as mellow as vinegar. Nothing and no one could make him any different. Certainly not the absence of one of his kids.

"He didn't mellow a damn bit, dumbass."

"I know." He squeezes his eyes shut.

"You could've looked back. You could've called. You could've acted like we still existed. You just took off, leaving everything and everyone, including us, behind you."

"I fucked up."

"Yep," I bark. "We've established that. Even though Dad was an asshole, we always had one another. But you, when you left, you made us feel like we didn't even have that."

Dylan hangs his head. "I'm sorry. There's nothing more I can say. All I can do is live my life every day, trying to make up for my mistake. I now know how precious time is. Ian taught me that. Ian made us closer than we ever were before. He made us stronger. And before he went in, he made us promise never to drift apart again."

"I didn't promise him that," I blurt out, angry at my brother.

"I know, but I did, and I'm never going to give up on you. If I could go back and do the time instead of you, I'd fucking do it in a heartbeat."

"I don't regret the time I did. I only regret that Ian's in there now."

Dylan scrubs his hand down the side of his face, stopping to scratch his beard. "That was his choice. But you gave him ten years of life he wouldn't have had otherwise."

"I can't get the image of him being led away in handcuffs out of my head," I admit and take a deep breath. The memory has been haunting me.

"Ian's tougher than he looks. Handcuffs are nothing compared to the shit he went through with his cancer. He is so much more than his illness. Luna made sure of it. She never left his side when he was sick, but once he was healthy, she made sure he got out and really lived every moment to the fullest."

"I'm happy he had someone in his life."

"Luna has her sights set on you," he warns me.

"I know." I lean back, resting my palms against the bed. "How do I get her to stop?"

Dylan laughs. "You can't. She may be the most stubborn person I've ever met. It's best to just give in."

"When did you become such a pussy?"

My brother's lip curls. "If loving a good woman makes me a pussy, I'll accept who I am. But when did you become such an asshole? You were never this guy."

"Prison teaches you not to be nice."

"Look around, Nevin." He lifts his arms, waving his hands. "You're not in prison anymore."

"No shit, but it's hard to change. I need more time to get used to being on the outside."

"Don't take too long, before you alienate all the people around you who want to help."

"Maybe I don't need help," I say, staying true to my asshole personality.

"We all need help, Nevin."

"Whatever," I mutter.

"Now," he says, rubbing his hands down his jeans, "Ro wants me to invite you over for dinner tonight. She said she won't take no for an answer, but beware, she's a shit cook. I'll do my best to order a pizza or something instead of choking down her slop."

I want to tell him no, but I'm fucking hungry, and the vending machine and the greasy diner across the street aren't doing it for me anymore.

"It would make Ro happy, and Luna will be there, of course. They rarely do anything without each other."

I raise an eyebrow. "Sex?"

Dylan shakes his head. "No, man. That shit isn't even funny."

"Didn't think it was funny, but it would be hot as fuck."

"They're sisters, jagoff."

I shrug. "Whatever. I'm hungry, so I'll come for the food."

But really, I want to see Luna. I want to talk to her about Ian and hear about the brother I barely know as an adult. What is he like? Is he really as happy as everyone makes him out to be?

"Doesn't matter why you come. All I know is Rosie will be happy. She was brought up believing family is everything. Be prepared to be sucked in by the Gallos."

"Oh, goodie," I mumble. "Sounds extremely dull."

"Nah, Nev. They're good people with good hearts. You'll see."

"I don't plan on hanging around."

"Are you leaving town?"

I shake my head. "No, but I have my own life to live. I'm not going to become a third wheel in your Gallo love affair."

"I don't want your ass at my house all the time. I enjoy my wife and my life. Luna's enough to deal with on a constant basis. I don't need to add another person."

"I'll come."

"Be there at six. I brought my bike over on my flatbed. You can use it as long as you need, unless you have other transportation."

"It's attached to me." I move my feet back and forth. "They haven't failed me yet."

"You get your license back?"

"Yep."

"Can't walk to my house." He pulls out a slip of paper from his pocket and sets it along with a key on the table next to him. "Takes about twenty minutes to get to our place."

"I'll be there," I tell him, but I don't move off the bed as I stare at the key.

When he moves toward the door, I say, "Dylan."

He stops moving and looks over his shoulder.

"Thanks, man."

He gives me a chin lift before opening the motel door and disappearing into the sunlight.

Holy shit. My brother is giving me his bike to use. That's a big move on his part. I know how much he loved his bikes, and no one was ever allowed to touch them. I haven't ridden a bike in ten years, and I'm not sure I even remember how.

I THROW on a pair of jeans and a T-shirt I picked up at the thrift store the other day, trying to look decent for my brother's uppity wife.

"Hi," Rosie says with a giant smile on her face.

"Hi."

She moves back, motioning for me to come inside. "I'm so happy you came."

"Sure," I mumble, kicking off my boots as soon as I'm in the foyer.

I look around, stunned by the size of my brother's place. He did well for himself. Not only is his wife high-class, his place is too.

"Luna's in the kitchen with Dylan, making some appetizers for us."

"Is she as good of a cook as you?" I ask Rosie.

She walks in front of me, swaying her fine ass. I'll give my brother that; he found himself a pretty chick with a smoking-hot body. "Your brother is the only one who makes anything that could be considered a decent meal. My sister and I are more about the pregame dinner experience."

"I can eat pretty much any horseshit."

"Then you've come to the right house," she says as

we walk into the kitchen, where Dylan and Luna are at the kitchen island, placing some tiny things on plates.

"Just in time," Luna says, greeting me with the warmest smile as she pulls off an oven mitt. "I hope you brought your appetite because we went a little crazy with all our favorite apps."

I soak it all in. The happy faces. The immaculate kitchen. The divine smell. It has been so long since I've been around anything even half as good as this.

"I did."

"Good," she says, grabbing a plate off the counter and heading my way.

"Beer?" Dylan asks as he stands in front of the fridge.

"Please."

Luna lifts the plate filled with tiny foods in front of me. "Try these. I made them just for you."

I stare at the tiny, round things, wondering what the fuck they are. As I reach forward, she pulls the plate back. "Any allergies? I should've asked before we started cooking, but I figured you would've had a fit."

"None. And I wouldn't have had a fit."

She stares at me.

"I wouldn't." My brother hands me a beer and shrugs.

"If you were allergic to something, we would've rolled with it," Luna says, thrusting the plate closer to my face.

"Only things rolling are these into my stomach," I

tell her, grabbing one of the little puffs from the white plate.

"It's filled with feta and spinach."

"Feta?"

"Cheese." She rolls her eyes like I'm a moron.

"Strong-ass cheese," Dylan adds. "Fancy shit we never had in the house as kids."

Luna and Rosie gasp in unison.

"You didn't have feta?" Luna asks my brother.

"We were lucky if we had a slice of that shit made from oil. Cheese was a luxury, and my dad wasn't going to spend his cash on something that wasn't necessary for survival," Dylan explains.

"But cheese is everything," Rosie tells him.

"These two are dramatic, yeah?" I ask Dylan.

He nods. "More than you know."

"Don't you like cheese?" Luna asks me as I stuff the pastry into my mouth and struggle to chew. The things are so hot, I'm not sure I'll have a taste bud left once I swallow.

"I do," I tell her with my mouth full as I jostle the pastry around with my tongue.

"How is it?" Luna asks, staring up at me with such hope.

I choke it down and somehow don't wince at the aftertaste the feta has left behind. "It's great," I lie. In this moment, I know I don't like feta, and nothing can change my mind. Not even the sweet piece of ass offering it to me.

"Good." She smiles, offering me more. "Have another."

I peer over at Dylan, and he's laughing his ass off. "It's different."

"Way."

She shakes the plate, and I grab another, wondering if I should just let it burn off my taste buds this time. If everything we eat tonight is like this feta shit, maybe it's better not to have any left on my tongue. But at least I have the beer to wash away the taste.

"Sit. Sit," Rosie says as she grabs something out of the fridge. "I made my guac and salsa. Luna said you loved it when she brought you some."

I look over at her, and she shrugs. She wasn't around when I ate it, quickly leaving before I had a chance to dig in. "It was some of the best I'd ever tasted."

"Good because I made a ton," she says, placing the biggest bowl of guacamole I'd ever seen in my life on the counter. "It's not something that keeps well either."

I try to push away the uncomfortable feeling I have being here. I feel like I don't fit in anywhere since I got out. Everyone moved on with their lives. Made something of themselves while I was stuck behind bars with my life on hold.

"How are you settling in?" Rosie asks me.

"Good."

"You're welcome to stay with us. We have a guest room that we never use."

"I'm comfortable where I am."

"Leave him be. He's happy where he is."

"No one's happy at the Wayward Traveler."

"That's not entirely true," Luna says. "I'm sure they have plenty of happy *customers*."

I lift my beer, knowing damn well there're plenty of happy people based on the sounds coming out of the rooms. "She's not wrong."

Rosie's face sours. "Our place is cleaner, though," she tells me as I fill my mouth with the best damn guac I've ever had.

"My room is clean. I scrubbed that bitch down the first day."

"Smart," Luna mutters as she grabs herself a beer from the fridge, bending in the most perfect way to give me a primo view of her ass and hips.

As I sit here, I think about how I've been acting. I've been pissed, taking it out on Luna, Dylan, and anyone else who's been around me. I'm not angry about prison. I made that choice to serve the time. I'm pissed that my brother is gone. But every person in this room, and many people not here, did everything they could to save his life.

They brought him joy, and all I've been doing is stealing any sliver of happiness they have. Ian would slap me upside the head if he were still here, telling me to stop being such a prick. He wouldn't be wrong.

"I appreciate the offer, Rosie. It's very nice of you, but you have your own life and I'm fine at the Wayward. I like having some space and privacy."

She smiles at me across the island. "If you ever change your mind, the bed's waiting."

"I have a spare bedroom too, you know," Luna adds. "I could use a roomie."

"I can't move in with you," I tell her, shocked she'd even make the comment casually.

"Why not? Ro used to live with me, but when she moved out, I didn't want to ask a stranger to live with me."

"I'm a stranger," I say, which isn't a lie.

She shakes her head. "You're not a stranger. You're my brother-in-law and my best friend's brother. Ian talked about you so much, I feel like I've known you forever."

"He talked about me?" I ask.

"All. The. Time. You were like his own personal superhero, Nevin."

I sit there, hand on my beer, stunned into silence for a moment. "I didn't do anything heroic."

"You gave him time and freedom. There's nothing bigger someone can do for another. He only said good things about you. I just want you to know you have options."

"I'll think about it," I mumble, trying to get her off my case. "I don't know if I could live with a chick. Shit would get complicated."

"Pick up your dirty underwear off the floor, and nothing will get complicated," she tells me.

"Don't wear any, remember?"

"Me either." She winks, and fuck me, my cock comes roaring to life more than it has since the day I stepped out into the fresh air.

I push away the attraction, thinking of the worst shit I can to get rid of my wood. "Right now, I'm good."

"Offer stands," she says, lifting another plate of apps and thrusting them toward me again. "Hanky panky?"

I blink, staring at her. "What?" Is she offering to make out with me in front of everyone?

"They're little pieces of bread with meat and cheese melted on top."

I let out the breath I'd been holding as I adjusted how I'm sitting to help my dick settle down. "Why not." I shrug, picking a tiny piece.

"I think some people call it shit on a shingle," Luna says.

"Looks like it," I tell her before shoving it into my mouth. But I'm instantly greeted by familiar tastes that are better than anything I've eaten in close to a decade.

"Those are good," my brother says. "Better than most of the fancy things these two like."

"We're not fancy, baby. Your taste in food is just bland."

"We ate to live, Ro. It wasn't about the taste or nutrition."

"Shameful," his wife mutters.

"Survival was everything," he explains.

"I lived on canned tuna for years," I tell them.

"I can't touch the shit anymore. Had it way too

much as a kid, and it left me with nothing but bad memories," Dylan adds.

"It was one of my staples at the commissary."

"How horrible," Luna says, frowning.

"Trust me. It was a treat compared to the slop they gave us," I tell her.

"Did they have food brought in?" Rosie asks.

My brother laughs. "I'm sure the meals were catered."

"The prisoners cooked everything. I couldn't even tell you what some of the stuff was sometimes. But I survived."

"What's the commissary?" Luna asks.

"Kind of like a prison store."

"Oh," she says, sliding onto the stool next to me. "That's interesting."

"Not really. It's all shit, but it's better shit than you could get as part of your free room and board."

She snorts. "You're kind of funny."

"You're so innocent," I reply.

Rosie bursts into laughter. "Don't let her cute face fool you. She's the devil in disguise."

"Doubtful," I tell her, wondering what it would be like to bang the fuck out of an innocent piece of ass like Luna Gallo.

"I'm an angel," Luna says, throwing one of the feta things at her sister.

Although I want nothing more than to fuck Luna Gallo, I know I can't risk ruining my brother's marriage.

I concentrate on the guac, trying not to stare at her slender, tanned legs as she sits next to me. Every time she shifts, I can't help but wonder how soft her skin is and what those thighs would feel like wrapped around my face until I suffocated.

I let them talk, nodding when I feel the time is right and grunting to add a little noise. But I keep my lips shut, soaking in all the information about them I can.

They are good people.

Too good for me.

9

LUNA

Nevin squints against the sunshine as he lifts his coffee cup to his lips. "We don't have to do this today. You probably have better things to do."

I shake my head. "I go in late tonight, and I have my whole afternoon free."

"And you said, let me help a stranger?" He doesn't release the cup as he stares across the table at me. "I'm sure you could've thought of something more fun to do with your free afternoon."

"Nope," I clip out. "Nothing makes me happier than being able to help."

"I could've done this myself," he lies.

I push the thin newspaper to the side. "You learned how to search the internet for job listings in the last twenty-four hours?"

"No," he grunts.

"Well, since most places don't put want ads in news-papers anymore, you're stuck with me until you're up-to-date on technology."

"Up-to-date?" he asks, tilting his head. "I was never up-to-date."

"Did you have a computer at home before?"

Nevin leans back, head still tilted and hand on his cup, staring at me across the table like I have two heads. "What do you think?"

I shrug. "Didn't everyone have a computer at home when we were in school?"

Nevin closes his eyes, smiling. "Babe, you think my dad cared enough about us to buy an expensive machine for us to play on?"

I grimace and swallow down my stupidity. "I just figured…"

"Don't assume anything when it comes to my child-hood because it's probably wrong."

"Sorry," I whisper, tucking some of the strands of hair that have fallen free behind my ear as I peer down at my computer screen. "I don't know what I was thinking."

There's awkward silence for a few seconds as I think about my next words. I avoid eye contact, knowing damn well I'll start babbling.

Just as I'm about to open my mouth, Nevin does first. "Thank you for this, though."

I peer up, surprised to hear him utter nice words. "You're welcome." I smile.

He smiles back before he gazes at my laptop. "Did you find anything for someone who has no skills and no work history?"

My smile slips for a second, but I catch myself and change course. I don't want him to lose hope. "Not yet, but I'm sure there's a job for someone like you."

"Sure," he mumbles.

"Do you have your high school diploma?"

He shakes his head. "Got sentenced before the start of second semester."

"Damn," I whisper.

I forgot he was so young when he was sent to prison. Wrapping my head around the fact that he wasn't even a legal adult when his father died makes it hard to come to terms with his being sent to an adult prison.

He leans forward, resting his arms on the table. "But I got my GED in prison."

"That's good," I say cheerfully, trying to focus on the positives. "It opens you up to more possibilities."

"Sure. I went from bagger to cashier lickety-split," he teases, turning his gaze on the window next to us, staring into the sunshine. "I'm a lucky son of a bitch."

I fill out the line about his education, working to complete his online profile. "Do you have any special skills?"

He doesn't answer right away and keeps his eyes trained on the world passing by outside the coffee shop. "I used to work on cars."

"What type of work?"

"I was learning to do custom auto paint before…"

"It's a skill for sure. Think you could still do it?"

He shrugs again. "Maybe, but I'd need some practice."

"My cousin owns an auto body shop. You can talk to him."

"Maybe," he grumbles, but I already know it's a no without his saying the word.

"What other skills do you have?"

"I can pick a lock."

I snap my head up as I move my eyes from the screen to Nevin's sun-filled face. "You can pick a lock?"

He nods. "Finn taught me."

I don't know why that surprises me, but it does. Nothing should anymore. "Unless you want to be a locksmith, I don't think it's something that'll come in handy."

He lifts his hand, scratching the stubble that's covering his jaw as he stretches. "Probably not."

"What else?" I ask, my fingers hovering over the keyboard.

"I can fight."

I stare at him, waiting for him to say he's kidding, but he doesn't. "And that would be handy for what?"

"Bouncer or security."

I nod. He's not wrong. "Added," I say as I type in a fancier term, referring to his ability as conflict de-escalation or remediation.

"Are you actually applying for jobs?"

"I am, but I'll also post your application for potential employers to look over when they're searching for people. Someone may find you even if we don't apply for their position."

"I'm sure everyone wants a man who's spent his entire adult life in prison."

"I'd hire you at the shop if you were an artist," I tell him.

His lips flatten as he stares at me. "You'd hire me out of pity, Luna. You don't count."

"I do too, and it wouldn't be out of pity. We're busy as hell, and I could use more time off."

"I can make a mean stick figure," he says teasingly, looking a little less grim.

"I wish people wanted them. I'd snap you up in a heartbeat to be the official stick figure guy for Inked."

"Things could change."

"Stranger shit has happened," I tell him. "Designs some people want blow my mind sometimes."

"Like what?" he asks, looking genuinely interested.

"A pickle."

"Someone put a pickle on their skin?"

I nod, laughing as I remember the weird guy who wanted the damn thing.

"What else?"

"I had a guy who wanted a hand on his dick so it looked like it was wrapped around and holding it."

His eyes widen. "Did you do it?"

I scrunch my nose, remembering how creepy the guy was and how he threw me a million vibes that made my skin crawl. "Um, no. I'm not holding his junk for hours for that ridiculousness."

"Does it ever get awkward?"

"All the time."

"What was your most awkward one that you actually ended up doing?"

I lean back in my chair and reach for my overly sugared coffee. "God, there've been so many strange ones. I don't even know where to start."

"I saw some interesting ones in prison." He shakes his head, scrubbing his hand across his face. "But almost everyone had names somewhere on their body."

"Names are the kiss of death."

"You think?" He raises an eyebrow. "I thought that was bullshit."

"How many relationships last forever, Nevin?"

He shrugs. "Not as many as people think."

"I've done a fuck-ton of name cover-ups. Nobody ever listens."

"How many, exactly, is a fuck-ton?" he teases.

"Enough to know that it's a bad idea, but I get paid to tattoo the same spot of skin twice."

"Sounds like a win-win."

"I'd rather get paid once and not have to try to cover up a big patch of black ink. It's always in black ink."

"My brother have Rosie's name on him?" Nevin asks.

"Not that I know of, unless it's somewhere I haven't seen and they did it when the shop was closed, but anything's possible."

"They seem like a solid couple."

"She's crazy about him."

"He seems pretty crazy about her too."

"They're good for each other," I tell him.

And they are. Rosie was always more uptight than me, and Dylan pushes her outside her comfort zone when it's necessary. Something I tried to do for years but wasn't as successful.

"You ever want that?" he asks, moving his coffee cup around in a small circle as he stares at me.

"No," I lie, but I do.

I never used to, though. I avoided relationships for years, using men like they were a dime a dozen and there solely for my enjoyment. I didn't care if I broke hearts, but I never led them on. I never lied about what I wanted or what we'd be to each other. Many guys thought they'd be the one to get me to change my mind. I don't know if they thought their dick was the magic one that would have me running down the aisle, but it never happened.

He dips his chin, raising an eyebrow again. "Really?"

"Do you?"

"Answering a question with a question?" He smirks.

"Why not?"

He laughs. "I don't know." He reaches back and

rubs his neck, grimacing. "Maybe someday. I don't even know how to date. The last girlfriend I had was when I was sixteen. I'm pretty sure things have changed."

"The basics are still the same," I assure him.

"Really?"

"I'm serious." I stare at him.

He takes a deep breath and crosses his arms. "Everything about being an adult on the outside feels so confusing and difficult."

"They should make a manual," I tell him.

"They need a manual for people coming out of prison and reentering society. Do you know how many end up going back?"

"Based on the question, I'm guessing a lot."

"A majority. The deck is stacked against us. Even though I didn't do the crime, who's going to hire me after spending so long in prison?"

"Don't tell them."

He stares at me. "Don't tell them?"

I nod. "Sure. Why not?"

"And where do I say I was since I have no work history and I'm in my midtwenties?"

"Taking care of a sick relative in another country."

He doesn't look the least bit amused by my excuse. "And when they run the background check, because I'm sure they all do now, and see I was in prison?"

I wince. "Fuck. I don't know. Explain what really happened, or ask my uncle about getting your record cleared, so it doesn't show up when they do run the background check."

He sits a little straighter in his chair. "They can do that?"

"I'm not sure they can, but they'd know if it's possible."

"It's probably expensive." He sighs. "I'll need some money."

"Well, let's find you a job, then." I point at my laptop screen.

"I could become a gigolo."

I glance up as he smirks at me. "Really?"

"No, not really." He laughs again, and I like this side of Nevin.

"I could loan you the money."

His headshake is immediate. "Never happening."

"You can pay me back a little at a time."

"Nope," he clips.

"Why not?"

"I'm not taking your cash."

I roll my eyes. "It's not going to put me in the poorhouse."

"I didn't say it would. But if I'm going to do it, I'm going to do it myself."

"Hardheaded," I whisper to myself. "You're just like Dylan."

"It's a man thing."

"It's a dumbass thing."

"Babe," he says sharply. "I have only a little pride

left. Don't kill it by giving me your money. I'll do it on my own."

"Impossible," I mutter. "Then let's find you a job, Mr. Pride. Maybe you'd like to bag groceries."

"I could do that," he replies. "How hard can it be?"

"I know the manager of the store near your place."

He shakes his head. "I don't want help."

"What do you call this?" I wave my hand in front of the computer. "I'm helping you now."

"If I get a job, I want it to be because of me, not because you called in a favor and will have to pay it back."

I glare at him. "I'm pretty sure Susan isn't going to ask for a favor."

"Susan? The manager is a chick?"

"Women can be managers too, Nevin. We do work."

"I didn't say you didn't. I know you have a job."

"I *own* part of a tattoo shop. I don't have a *job*. I'm a business owner with a career."

He throws his hands up in front of himself. "I got it. Sorry, babe. Didn't mean to insult you."

I turn the laptop toward him, figuring if he wants to do it on his own, he can click a few buttons. "I filled everything out. Now you need to find the positions you want and click to submit an application for each one."

He stares down at the machine like it's going to bite him. "What the hell happened to using pen and paper?"

"This is easier."

"For whom?"

"It's called progress, buddy. Progress," I say very slowly.

He moves his fingers across the trackpad, moving slowly. "I don't like this."

He ignores me, busy watching the arrow on the screen. I stare at him, studying as he tries to get the hang of the trackpad. He doesn't complain too much, only grumbling a few times. A few clicks later, he pushes the laptop back my way.

"Done."

"Done?" I ask, placing my coffee back on the table.

"Yep. I applied to five jobs. They're all shit, but they'll do to get some cash in my hands."

"Anything is a place to start," I tell him, trying to be upbeat, but I know he has an uphill battle in front of him.

"Ian left me a little cash to get me started. It's how I pay for the Wayward, but the money won't last forever."

"I was serious about a roommate."

He stares at me with a blank expression. "Not happening."

"Why not?"

"Babe," he says slowly.

"Babe what?"

"No. I need to be alone. It's sweet of you, but I'm going to have to pass."

"Offer still stands. I'm barely home."

"I don't want to walk around smelling like roses and baby powder."

"Roses?" I ask, trying not to laugh at his ridiculous statement.

"Whatever that good-smelling shit you're wearing is."

I touch my neck, knowing I didn't put anything on this morning. "I smell good?"

He nods. "Better than good."

I smile, liking that he thinks I smell better than good. "I don't think it would rub off on you."

"Are you kidding me?"

"No."

"I'm sure it's in the air at your place. I'd walk out of there leaving a trail of flowery air behind me." He shakes his head. "Not a good look for a guy like me."

I roll my eyes again. "That's absurd."

He lifts his hands this time as he shrugs. "It's the truth. I've smelled my brother. He doesn't smell like Dylan, but he sure as hell smells like Rosie."

"That's because he rubs on her like he's a cat in heat. It's not because he walked through her air."

"Whatever you say," he says, not believing a word that just came out of my mouth.

"Maybe you'll change your mind."

"Doubtful."

I stare at him, and he stares back, but his gaze becomes a little too much.

"Well, I have to head to the shop. Want to come?"

"No."

I exhale, feeling a little relieved.

"I got shit to do."

"What?" I ask.

"Shit."

I stop myself from rolling my eyes, but it's hard. "Got it."

"Thanks for your help."

"Anytime. You need anything else, let me know."

He stands first, throwing a ten on the table, but I push it back before he has a chance to move. "I got it."

"Take it," he insists, pushing it back in my direction.

"I already paid."

"Well, now I'm paying you for paying."

I want to push it back at him, but I can see the man has pride...too much of it, actually. "Fine. Thank you."

"You can get the next one," he says to me.

"Deal." I smile.

He smiles back, looking bigger as he hovers over the table where I sit.

"Let me know if you get a call."

"A call?"

"From one of the applications."

He nods. "You got it. Talk soon."

"I hope," I say to him, thinking I'll hear from him soon.

I watch Nevin as he walks to the door, punches it open, and stops in the sunlight to peer up at the sky. He wants to be nice. He tries, but it's not natural for him. He's had to fight for everything in his life. He's scrappy and rough, but over time, I can see him softening a bit just like Dylan did.

I have hope for him, just like Ian does. Nevin deserves a little slice of happiness, and I'll do whatever I can to make sure he gets it.

10

NEVIN

"FUCK," I MUTTER UNDER MY BREATH WHEN SHE WALKS into the bar dressed to the nines, making my cock ache instantly. It's been two weeks since she helped me with my applications, all of which never panned out.

I didn't call her, even though she expected me to. I didn't want her to help me any more than she already had. I've taken up enough of her time, and the more I am around her, the more I want her. And in my brother Dylan's eyes, that is a huge issue.

My first night on the job and she has to stroll in here, looking good and probably smelling even better. She's with Rosie, smiling as they talk, until she starts to walk my way and her gaze lands on me.

Her smile falls in an instant. I did that. I hate myself for it too, but I know that, in the long run, it is for the best.

"You're working here now?" Luna asks, sliding onto a barstool across from me.

"I am," I tell her, continuing to wipe down the glass I pulled from the washer a minute ago.

"I'm surprised," Luna replies.

"Better than nothing," I tell her, keeping my eyes on her. "What do you two want to drink?"

"Two Coronas and two tequila shots," Rosie finally says, entering the conversation but changing the topic.

I set down the clean glass and reach into the cooler, pulling out two beers and twisting off the tops.

"Why here, though?" Luna pries, leaning forward on her stool, showing off her cleavage. "Didn't any of the places call?"

"It's the only place in town that would hire me on the spot." I slide the beers in front of the girls, offering them limes, but am waved off. "The others wanted a background check. Didn't want to deal with that shit."

"I'm sure they're happy to have you," Luna says, smiling at me like my lack of calling didn't wound her a little.

"I could give a shit if they're happy. Just need some cash to get back on my feet," I tell her before reaching for the tequila and pouring their shots.

"Thanks," Rosie says as I place the shots in front of them.

"No problem. Anything else?"

Rosie shakes her head.

"We're good for a bit," Luna answers. "But check on us when we get low."

I wander down the bar, not wanting to spend too much time with my sister-in-law and her hot-ass sister who's filled with sunshine and is making me her personal pet project.

"He's cold as ice," Rosie says to Luna as they clink their bottles together. "Let that one go, babe."

"I can't," Luna says. "I like him."

They're not looking at me and I'm not looking at them, but the way the sound carries behind the bar, I might as well be standing right in front of them.

"Why in God's name do you like him?"

Luna shrugs. "I have a feeling about him, Ro."

"Keep it friendly," Rosie warns her.

"Did you listen to anyone about Dylan?" Luna throws back before taking a sip of beer.

"The Walshes are complicated, but Dylan was different."

"Nevin's different too."

A woman I didn't even meet until a few weeks ago has defended me more than most people I've encountered in my life. And I've done nothing but be a miserable prick to her too.

"I don't think I'll ever get used to this new side of Luna. Where did the do-crazy-shit-and-fuck-all-the-people side of you go?"

Luna's face falls. "My best friend went to prison. He doesn't even look like himself anymore, but..." Luna stops talking, glancing down the bar at me as I pretend to be busy.

Rosie covers Luna's hand with hers as I watch from the corner of my eye, pretending not to be listening in on their conversation. "I get it. I really do. But you need to find your joy again, and I don't think Nevin's the way to do it."

"I've never needed a man to make me happy, Ro. You know that better than anyone."

"You've always been the badass out of the two of us."

I don't know why, but that statement makes me smile.

"Hey, handsome. Can I get another?" a woman asks, lifting her glass into the air to show me she's empty.

I pour her another whiskey sour and place it in front of her. "Do I know you?" she asks as her eyes wander around my face but never focus completely. "I know I do, but don't know from where."

By the stench of whiskey coming off her, I'm pretty sure she wouldn't be able to place her own face even if she were staring in the mirror.

"Nope. Never met you," I tell her, quickly finding something to keep myself away from the person I think is the local barfly and drunk. There's no doubt in my mind that she's a regular.

She lifts her glass, pointing at me with her finger as she fists the drink. "You were in the paper."

"Wasn't me," I mutter.

"Yeah. Yeah." She nods, almost spilling her drink over the side of her hand with her jerky movements. "You're the boy who went to prison for a crime he didn't commit."

Fuck. This is the worst part about living in a small town. The gossip. When there isn't much to talk about, everything becomes worthy of a story.

"You must have me confused with someone else." I try to get her to drop it, but as inebriated as she is, she doesn't catch on.

"It was you." She squints, focusing on my face so intently, you'd think she was seeing triple. "Solid thing you did for Ian. He's a great guy. Best bartender and listener there was this side of town."

"I'm nothing like him."

She laughs. "You can say that again. You're a light pour and not much of a talker either, but that'll change when you settle in."

Doubtful, but I'm not going to argue with her.

"Is it weird to be in his spot?" She keeps prying.

It seems to be the story of my life. I am always filling in for Ian. The bar had an opening because they hadn't been able to fill his position since he turned himself in. Enter me. A man looking for any type of employment, even a shitty bartender job at the worst drinking hole in town.

"No, ma'am. Just doing a job."

"Nevin." Luna's voice carries down the bar, and I glance her way, wanting to be rescued from the woman with so many wrinkles on her face, she obviously worships the sun.

I stalk away from whiskey sour and head toward the girls, being greeted by their smiling faces. The tequila has no doubt already started working its magic.

"Can you get us another, please?" Rosie asks as Luna stares at me, blinking slowly.

I give them a quick refill and am about to walk away when Luna asks, "You want to come to our grandparents' house for dinner next week?"

"No," is my swift and immediate answer.

"Why not?"

I lean over on one arm, getting close to the girl who could be a beauty queen. "Pretty sure they don't want people who did time in their home."

She giggles, slapping the bar. "You clearly don't know my family."

"You'd be right, but I remember they weren't fans of my family."

"They like Dylan," Rosie interjects. "Big fans of him."

"Shocking," I grumble. "But then again, Dylan was a suck-up."

Rosie pushes her long hair behind her shoulder, growing rigid. "He's not a suck-up."

"Ass-kisser sound better?" I ask, being a total dickhead.

"What's wrong with you?" Rosie asks me.

"I lack people skills." I shrug.

"I ain't buying your act, Nevin Walsh," Luna says in a no-nonsense tone.

"No act," I tell her. "I am, indeed, an asshole."

She leans forward, getting in my space. "A man who's an asshole wouldn't serve prison time for his brother."

I open my mouth to shoot something back her way, but I have nothing. I'd like to think most people would do it, but none of my other brothers would have for Ian, and they sure as shit wouldn't do that for me.

"Cat got your tongue?" she says in a teasing way with a smile that could light up the darkest room.

"They tried to pin it on me first, and I didn't lead them to believe otherwise."

"But you did the time," Luna says with a smug smile. "When we know damn well the others wouldn't have. You're a good man."

I grimace. "I'm not good, Luna. I don't know how many times I have to go over this with you. Ian is the good one, not me."

"You're right. Ian is a good man, Nevin. But he's still the one who hit your father in the head. You need to stop thinking of yourself as a criminal and recognize you're a hero in this situation."

Hero is a word that's never been used to describe me, and nothing they say or do will convince me otherwise.

"Oh, for fuck's sake," Rosie mutters under her breath.

"What?" Luna asks her with round eyes, looking so fucking sweet and innocent. "Where's the lie, Ro? Would you let me sit in prison if you did something and I took the rap for it?"

"No."

"There ya go." Luna waves her hand at Rosie. "I know Ian was sick, but you didn't know how sick he was. Yet you protected him when no one else did. End of story."

"Walsh!" the bar owner yells across the room. "Are you working or flirting?"

"I got to go," I tell them, grumbling under my breath about the prick who's now my new boss.

"Next Sunday. Dinner," Luna says before I can stalk away.

"Not happening," I tell her and make a quick exit, not having the time to argue.

An hour passes, and Luna and Rosie don't move off the stools. I've given them each one more beer and no more shots.

"We have to go, Lu. Dylan's coming to get us." Rosie slides off the stool and grabs her purse.

"I'm not leaving."

Rosie glares at Luna. "I'm not leaving you here."

"Been here plenty of times alone, Ro. I'm fine. I'll call a ride when I'm ready to leave."

Rosie leans over and says something in Luna's ear.

"Got it. I promise I'll text when I get home."

Rosie looks down the bar at me and waves before

glancing back at her sister. I don't know if it's a signal, like I'm supposed to look out for her twin, but I give her a quick chin lift as a goodbye.

Rosie stalks out of the bar as Luna grabs a bowl of peanuts that were left nearby and goes to town on them. She uses her dark-gray fingernails to pry each one open, dropping the shell into an empty glass.

Within sixty seconds, a man slides onto the stool her sister vacated.

Luna doesn't even look at him as he talks to her, his body facing her direction. He's half smashed, having been here for more hours than she has and drinking at a faster clip.

I don't know if it's how close he's sitting to her or the way her body's leaning away from him, but the hair on the back of my neck stands on end. I move a few feet closer, giving her space, but not giving him more than necessary.

"Come on, Luna You know I can make you feel good," he says to her, slurring every few words.

"We've been over this before, Oliver. It's still a hard no." She tosses another shell into the glass, staring straight ahead, looking like she isn't affected by his presence. "Never going to happen, just like the fifty other times you've hit on me."

He touches her arm, but she doesn't move. "Baby, I got the cure for your sadness. Lemme help work that anger out of you."

I turn toward them, watching and listening, ready to pounce.

She glances down at his legs. "There ain't nothing in your pants that's going to put a smile on my face. You may as well move on and stop wasting your time and mine."

I chuckle softly. She's spunky with that side of sunshine. I like that in a chick. Maybe she isn't all rainbows like I thought when she came by my room a few weeks ago.

She lifts her beer to her lips, ignoring the guy. But he doesn't take the hint. He keeps going, and with every passing second, I'm growing more impatient.

"Why don't we get out of here and find a place where we can be alone?" he says, running his finger up her arm.

She doesn't move, but she glances down where his skin is touching her flesh. "You have thirty seconds to remove your finger from my arm, or the only place you're going is the emergency room."

He laughs, and while he thinks she's kidding, I suddenly have no doubt she could break his finger in a heartbeat. I remember Luna's father, and although he's an asshole, I would put money on the fact that he taught his three daughters how to protect themselves when they ran into slimeballs.

"Baby, why do you gotta be so cold?" he asks her, not taking the hint or removing his finger. "Is it because your boy toy Ian isn't here?"

As if I'm watching in slow motion, Luna snaps, reaching over with her other hand and taking his index finger in her grip. "I asked you nicely to fuck off," she says, bending his finger back in the most unnatural way until it busts.

He lurches forward, trying to follow her motion so his finger doesn't snap clean off. "Please," he begs like a little bitch.

Even though I'd like nothing more than to watch her continue to manhandle the asshole, I step around the bar and grab him by the collar. "Out you go, fucker," I tell him, hauling his ass off the stool.

"Mind your own fucking business!" he hollers, twisting and trying to fight me off.

"When you touched her, it became my business." I drag him with the heels of his shoes scraping against the sticky wooden floor. As soon as I make it to the door, I kick it open and push him outside. "Next time I see your face, I'll beat your ass."

"You're a little bitch!" he yells, backing away from me when I move forward.

I cross my arms over my chest and glare at him. "Try it, buddy."

"Dickhead." He gives me the middle finger with the hand Luna didn't mangle before he jogs away into the darkness. I wait a full minute before going back inside, waiting to see if he'll try anything.

"You didn't have to do that," Luna says as soon as I'm back behind the bar. "I had him handled."

"Literally," I mutter with a small laugh. "But it's my job, Luna. Don't need guys in here bothering the customers."

My reply doesn't put a smile on her face. I didn't haul him out because I'm paid to do it; I took his ass out because he was bothering her, and none of it sat well with me.

"Well, at least you're doing your job," she tells me with a sour look.

"Don't move from that seat until you're ready to go," I tell her, pointing at her spot.

"And who made you the boss of me?" she asks.

"Ian."

11

LUNA

A WOMAN ONLY HAS SO MUCH PATIENCE, AND MINE IS quickly running out.

I can understand Nevin being bitter after wasting his life in prison, but he made that choice, and he's finally free. Now, he's hell-bent on making everyone pay, including me.

"You're an asshole." I hop off the stool, so filled with hurt that if my drink were full, I'd throw it in his face.

"You keep telling me that, and I never deny it."

I grab my purse and pull out a fifty, which is more than enough to cover our tab and way too generous of a tip for such a miserable prick. "You can keep being mad at the world, but it won't change anything except making everyone around you as miserable as you are."

"Let me call you a cab," he offers without an apology, as if we aren't in the middle of a fight.

"I can get myself home. I've survived this long without your help," I snap.

"Luna." He takes a step forward, but we're still separated by the bar.

I put up my hand, done with him. "Save it."

"Please."

I shake my head, barely able to stand still with the amount of anger welling up inside me. "I hope you enjoy your misery. It'll be the only thing to keep you company for a while," I tell him, throwing down my money before heading toward the door.

"Luna!" Nevin yells as I punch the door handle, taking out my feelings on the hard piece of metal. "Wait."

But I don't stop moving.

Fuck him.

How dare he throw Ian's name in my face. I've done nothing to him except try to help and be someone for him to lean on, but no more.

As soon as I'm in the parking lot, I order a ride home and pace in front of the building like a wild animal.

"Asshole," I mutter to myself, curling my lip. "I'm sorry, Ian. I can't do it." I lift my face toward the sky, soaking in the stars dotting the firmament above. "I tried, and now he's on his own. I'm done."

The door to the bar swings open, and Nevin stalks out, looking more pissed off than I am, and that's saying something because I'm stabby. "I said wait," he barks, huffing loudly.

I shrug a shoulder, pretending not to give two shits. "Who do you think you are? You don't get to order me around and think I'll listen!" I shout, curling my fists at my sides, wishing I could pop him one to knock some damn sense into him.

He groans, dragging his hand down his face. "Women are fucking impossible."

I laugh, sounding a bit crazy, but I don't care. "I'm impossible?" I touch my chest, jerking my head back. "I'm impossible?" I ask again, this time louder. "You're the one who's impossible."

"Do you ever stop talking?"

"I may talk a lot, but—"

He advances, grabbing my face, and hauls me forward. I don't have time to react before his lips are on mine, kissing me hard and deep and making my knees go weak.

My body sways forward as if I crave his touch and have been waiting for this moment my entire life. My brain doesn't have time to process what's happening, but my body does, and it's decided to lean into him and take whatever he's going to give me.

The world around us ceases to exist as the air grows thick, but all I can smell is Nevin, and all I feel is him too. My hands find his stomach, resting on the hard muscles of his abdomen. The heat from his body soaks through his thin T-shirt, warming my palms.

Tiny goose bumps break out across my skin when he slides one of his hands to the back of my head, tangling his fingers in my hair. Without thinking, I tilt my head, opening my mouth wider to his forceful kiss.

For a man who hasn't kissed anyone in damn near a decade, he sure can make a girl's toes curl.

This isn't good.

Not good at all.

Before I can push him away, he pulls back, ending the kiss. I instantly miss his heat. "Holy shit," I whisper, winded by the crazy-stupid kiss, and I nearly double over, hyperventilating.

When I peer up, Nevin looks as shocked as I feel about the entire situation. "I'm sorry," he says softly, and it's the first time one of his apologies has sounded sincere.

I touch my lips as I straighten my back, facing him. "Why would you do that?" I ask, finally coming to terms with the reality that he kissed me.

Nevin Walsh kissed me, and it wasn't chaste.

"I just…" He runs his fingers through his hair, blowing out a long breath. "I thought…"

"Were you trying to shut me up?"

He shakes his head. "What? No! Fuck it," he snaps and spins around. "This was a mistake." And with that final blow, he stalks back into the bar, leaving me staring at the door in disbelief.

"Motherfucker," I hiss, feeling like the man slapped me square in the face.

A *mistake*.

He said I was a mistake.

Our kiss was a mistake.

Well, fuck him. It sure didn't feel like a mistake when he was kissing me so hard my knees wobbled.

No one—and I mean no one—has ever made that happen.

My car pulls up as my fingers touch the front door handle, ready to go back inside to give Nevin Walsh another piece of my mind.

I kick the cinders in the parking lot and pull my hand back to my side, spinning to the car. "He's not worth it."

The second I walk into my apartment, I rip off my top, unhook my bra, and toss it on the couch before stripping off the rest of my clothes. A shower never sounded as good as it does now. Nevin's scent clings to me as a constant reminder of his cruelty when he walked away from me, leaving my lips buzzing from the kiss.

My butt hasn't even hit the couch cushion after my shower before there's a knock at the door. I don't move as I stand in my living room wearing nothing except a thin tank top and shorts that are so short, the bottoms of my ass cheeks hang out. I glance around, looking for something, anything to cover up with.

"Who is it?" I yell out in a panic as I grab a fuzzy pink throw blanket off the couch and wrap it around my middle section like a bath towel.

"Open up, Luna."

Ah. The asshole.

"Go away, Nevin. I have nothing to say to you, and you sure as hell have nothing I want to hear."

"Just open up," he pleads in a softer tone. "Please."

I chew on my thumbnail, having an internal war with myself about letting him inside. We're like oil and water. Nothing between us has been easy, and we've only known each other for a few short weeks. He's the most infuriating man I've ever met, and that's saying something because every male in my family is a total pain in the ass.

I walk across the room and stand close to the door. The last thing I need is for the entire apartment complex to hear our conversation. Nosy bitches. "Why should I?"

"I'm an asshole," he mutters loud enough for me to hear.

"Tell me something I don't already know."

"We need to talk."

"We have nothing to say to each other."

"I'll stand out here all night, Lu."

"It would serve you right."

He deserves some time to think about his actions, or at least the words he uses. He can't be an asshole one minute and think I'll easily forgive him the next. That's not the way it works in my world.

I open the door, finding him with his hands on the frame, leaning forward. His head pops up, and his eyes meet mine.

"Listen, buster," I start, standing tall and using my firm, I-mean-business tone but keeping my hand on the door to block him from coming inside. "I get you're pissed off. You spent a good chunk of your life in prison and you don't have shit to your name, but that doesn't give you the right to be mean to me and take out all your pissed-off aggression on me either. You want to be a dick, go be a dick to someone else. You want a friend, you know where I am, and I'll be that friend. But stop thinking you can walk all over me and I'll be here as that carpet for you to wipe your shoes on while you're figuring out the rest of your life."

I take in a sharp breath, winded from the long diatribe I nailed with perfect execution. I haven't moved a muscle, keeping my feet planted in the doorway, and to my shock, Nevin hasn't moved either.

His fingertips are white, curling around the molding of the doorframe. "You done?"

I nod, finally letting go of the door to cross my arms. "I could keep going..."

He shakes his head as he takes one hand off the door and runs his thick fingers through his even thicker hair. I expect him to start talking right away, but in true Nevin fashion, he blows out a long, drawn-out breath first. "I like you."

I blink a few times and tilt my head. "Excuse me?"

"I. Like. You."

"Okayyyyy," I say, tilting my head a little more. "And?"

He glances up at my porch light before bringing his dark-green eyes back to mine. But this time, they're not filled with anger; they're brimming with fire. "You're not getting me, Luna. I want you. I want you more than I've ever wanted another person in the world. That kiss was…"

My first reaction is to tell him he's full of shit, but based on the look in his eyes, I believe he's telling me the truth. "But I'm a mistake," I say, throwing his earlier words in his face. "I know I didn't hear you wrong."

He takes a step forward, and I take a step back. "I feel like I'm living Ian's life. His job and now his girl."

"I wasn't and have never been your brother's girl. We are friends, Nev. Only friends."

Nevin lifts his hand, placing his rough palm against my cheek. I nearly melt into his touch, loving the warmth of his skin against mine. "If he were out, would I be here?"

"If he were out, you'd still be in prison."

"If he were out, would he be here right now?" he asks again.

I shake my head and stare into those smoldering green eyes that are the color of a turbulent sea. "We didn't hang out all the time, and your brother was always on the move. No doubt, he'd have his face buried between—"

Nevin grabs me, crushing his lips against mine. But this time, unlike before, I instantly melt into him. I dig my fingers into his T-shirt, holding on for dear life, never wanting this feeling to end.

NEVIN

MY PHONE BUZZES FOR THE FIFTH TIME IN UNDER A minute. I roll over, unable to ignore the constant barrage of noise in my sleep. I worked a ten-hour shift last night at the bar, slinging drinks and dealing with drunk, self-absorbed assholes all night.

It's been a week since I kissed Luna, and I've been doing my best not to shut her out. I'm still trying to find my way in a world I don't really understand, but Luna's been helping me with more shit than I'm really comfortable with.

Luna: Hey.

Luna: What are you doing?

Luna: Nevin.

Luna: You awake?

Luna: NEVIN!!!

"Fuckin' Luna," I whisper, sliding my finger over the screen to reply to her before she sends another text.

Or worse yet, marches her ass over here and hauls me out of bed.

She's been stuck to me like glue lately. True to her word, or maybe not, she is, in fact, making me a pet project.

Me: Yeah?

I close my eyes, hoping she's found something else to occupy her time so I can get more sleep. Of course, I'm wrong, and she's done no such thing.

Luna: Come to dinner today.

Me: I don't think it's a good idea.

Luna: It is. My grandparents want you there.

Me: Doubtful.

Luna: My grandmother will be insulted.

Me: She will not.

Luna: You don't like home-cooked food, do you?

Dylan told me the Gallo family is nothing like we thought growing up. If Luna and Rosie are any indication, I'd say we were not only wrong, but dead fucking wrong. We always thought of them as uppity and too good for us—or even most people—but that couldn't be further from the truth.

Every week, I've been invited to Sunday family dinner, but it is becoming harder and harder to come up with excuses.

Luna: I'm coming to pick you up.

Me: Give me an hour.

"Fuck," I hiss again, jumping up from my bed to

shower. The stench of musty cigarettes and sour beer clings not only to my clothes, but to my skin too.

Luna: Yay! I'll give you ten minutes so you can't change your mind.

Before I hop in the shower, I shoot off a text to Dylan, letting him know I'm coming to dinner.

Dylan: Fucking finally.

My stomach tightens at the thought of being surrounded by so many people. When individuals say something shitty or send me that judging look, I know how to handle them alone. But an entire family, all passing judgment about my life and actions without knowing the full truth—it is a little too much and too soon.

Me: I'm not staying long.

Dylan: You will.

Me: No, man. I'm not good with that many people. And why are you being nice?

Dylan: Dessert is the best part. Can't leave until you've had that. And we're brothers, dumbass.

Me: I don't like sweets, and what does that matter?

Dylan: Don't tell Grandma. She'll be devastated. Choke it down if you must, but do not leave beforehand. She'll be insulted.

Me: Why do you want me there? You've made it clear to stay away from Luna.

Dylan: She's still off-limits, but that doesn't mean I don't want you around.

I grunt, hating that I have to pretend for a group of

people I don't know. But not only will this make Luna happy, it'll make Rosie and Dylan happy too. They've been up my ass constantly about spending more time with her family. I've avoided the topic as long as possible, but now, my time is officially up.

I toss my phone onto the bed, thinking everyone in my life is insane. I don't know what the hell happened while I was in prison, but something shifted. Most of my brothers are still assholes, but Dylan embraces his wife's family like he's been a member for his entire life.

I make quick work of the shower, washing off the stank of last night and trying to make myself presentable for Luna, Rosie, Dylan, and the family I spent most of my life both envying and despising.

I barely have my body toweled off when Luna walks through the front door of my tiny apartment without knocking.

Her eyes land right on me as I walk out of the bathroom in only a towel.

"Well...I..." She blinks before her eyes travel down and then up, soaking in my barely covered body. "You..."

I'm just as shocked as she is. Not only because I'm half dressed, but also because she walked right in like she pays the rent, and she is also tongue-tied, which is something I've never seen happen to her before.

"You good?" I ask her, smirking because she's staring.

She nods, her eyes glued to my pecs with utter fascination. She swallows, blinking a few more times before she seems to find her words. "Very."

I don't bother moving, liking the look on her face. "You look like you've never seen a half-dressed man before, Lu, which I know isn't true."

She shakes her head. "Just caught me off guard, is all. I see you're not ready."

"You didn't give me much warning," I tell her, adjusting my towel so it doesn't fall, although I'd love to see her reaction.

Luna's feet finally come unstuck from the spot near the door, and she moves toward the couch, looking everywhere except at me. "You always have a reason you can't make it. Figured I'd make it impossible for you to find a new excuse."

I rub my forehead and sigh. "I'm doing this for you."

"And yourself."

"How's that?" I ask.

She smiles as she leans back, getting more comfortable. "My grandma makes the best food. When was the last time you had a great home-cooked meal?"

"Dad wasn't much of a cook, and neither was my mom, so that would be never."

She frowns immediately. "That's sad. Everyone should have that."

"I'd prefer if you cooked me the meal rather than going to your family's weekly dinner."

Luna shakes her hand and laughs. "You want to die before you have a real chance to live?"

"Not preferable."

"Then you don't want to eat my food. I make great apps, but you can't live on them forever. I tried. Trust me, I tried."

"I'm sure you can make more. You've lived this long somehow."

"Rice, ramen, and pizza rolls are my means of survival. Other than that, I'm shit out of luck besides restaurants, but that gets old after a while." She clears her throat as her gaze travels down my body again. "You should probably wear something else to dinner, though."

"You don't think they'd like this look?" I motion toward the towel hanging from my waist.

She giggles, and it's the most glorious sound. Something she hasn't done enough of since I've met her. "The women will approve. The men will not."

I nod. "Got it. Clothes."

"Nothing dressy. Jeans and a T-shirt are fine."

"Well, that's all I have."

"We should go shopping tomorrow."

I groan. "Can't you buy the shit for me? Please," I beg. "Spare me a trip to the mall."

She shakes her head, loving to torment me. "No way, Nev. I need to see how the clothes fit on your body."

I grumble, but spending time with Luna is no hardship. The woman is smoking hot even if she's a pain in the ass at times, but what woman isn't? If she wants to spend the day with me, I am all about it.

"Now, go get dressed. Grandma does not like when we're late."

"Can I call her something else?"

Luna smiles, lighting up my dingy, tiny apartment. "Sure thing, bud. Call her Mrs. G or Maria. She's flexible, but if she doesn't like what you're calling her, she will let you know. We don't hold our tongues."

"Fucking great," I mutter.

"Now, scoot," she says, waving her hands at me.

THIRTY MINUTES LATER, we're walking through the front door of one of the biggest houses I've ever seen, let alone stepped inside. I feel very underdressed and somehow not clean enough either, even though I just showered.

The Gallos don't just have a little money. Based on the size of the place, they have tons of money and aren't afraid to spend it either.

"We're here!" Luna yells out as I'm kicking off my boots.

"Back here!" someone yells, but there's so much noise, I barely catch the words.

When I don't move right away, Luna takes my hand. She turns and smiles at me before she tugs me ever so slightly forward, and I follow. I don't know where to look first as my gaze moves from one flashy, expensive thing to the next.

Every room, wall, and item in the house is gorgeous. I never believed people really lived like this. Growing up, I thought that was all made up for television, and it still feels like a lie until moments like these.

"Nevin," a sweet old woman says, walking toward me with her arms outstretched like she wants... "It's so nice to meet you." She wraps those same arms around me, hugging me tightly before I have a chance to finish my thought or brace myself for the impact.

"It's nice to meet you too, ma'am," I tell her, still holding Luna's hand and using my other hand to hug her grandmother back.

She backs up, smiling at me with her beautiful eyes. Even with her age, I can see her beauty and features I've studied so many times on Luna's face. "I want you to make yourself at home, and I hope you brought your appetite with you."

"Yes, ma'am."

"Dinner will be ready in a bit. Everyone's out back or in the family room. Luna," her grandmother says, turning to the girl stuck to me like glue. "Introduce Nevin to everyone and show him around. Don't let him leave this house hungry."

"Impossible, Grams. I'll make sure to send him home with leftovers too."

"Perfect," her grandmother says, touching Luna's face softly before walking away.

"She's sweet," I say, watching her as she heads to the back of the house where I assume the kitchen is.

I can't imagine growing up with someone like that in my life. Would I be different from how I am now? I can't imagine her grandmother standing by, letting one of her grandchildren be beaten on the regular like we were. Hell no. She'd keep them safe. She'd love them even if no one else would.

"The absolute best, but everyone in my family is."

"You're not partial or anything," I tease her.

"They're solid. I'd think that too if they weren't my people... All of them except my father. He's a little more..."

"Assholish," I quickly add, earning myself a scowl.

Luna hooks her arm through mine again, not fazed by what I called her father. I like her this close. I like it way more than I should. "I was going to say protective or standoffish, but only when it comes to my sisters and me," she says, moving me toward the voices which are growing louder with every step.

There are people literally everywhere—on the couch, all over the floor, in every chair, and at every table—talking to one another in constant chatter.

"Are you related to all these people?" I ask her, glancing around.

"Yep. All of them," she says with a sigh, but I can tell she's proud. "It's exhausting sometimes."

My entire family consisted of my brothers and my father. No one else talked to us, and rightfully so. My father was an asshole. No one wanted to be around him, especially us, but we didn't have a choice until that night when we finally had had enough.

"Don't worry. You get used to being around so many people."

Doubtful.

My brother is right in the thick of the crowd as if he's been here his entire life instead of being a new addition. I'm envious of his ease with strangers.

When I look to Dylan's right a few people down, my gaze lands right on Luna's father. He's staring directly at me, and he's giving me the same look he did when I was a kid.

This should be interesting.

NEVIN

"HERE WE GO," I MUTTER AS HE STALKS TOWARD US.

"Relax," Luna says like it's no big deal. "He's harmless."

What the hell does she see when she looks at him? Does he come off like a big teddy bear to his kids? Because to everyone else who lays eyes on the guy, they can see the waves of asshole rolling off him like the ocean during a hurricane.

"Mr. Gallo," I say, keeping my chin high.

Show no fear.

"Nevin." He stares at me with his eyes slightly narrowed.

"It's nice to see you again, sir," I lie, which earns me a hand squeeze from Luna.

"You, too. I'm sorry about your brother. Ian's a good kid. He doesn't deserve to sit in prison."

Does this mean I did deserve it?

There's no animosity or hostility toward me like there used to be when I was a kid. "He is one of the good ones," I reply.

His gaze drops to where Luna has her hand hooked in my arm near my elbow. I'm ready, waiting for the blowback from the harmless gesture. "If you ever need to talk, I'm always here," he says, but this time, he's looking at me like I'm any other person in the room.

"Thank you, sir."

"You're a good kid too, Nevin. Not many would do what you did for your brother. Earned all my respect, giving up years of your life to save your brother."

I swallow, choking back the thickness in my throat. "You would've done the same."

He nods. "I would've in a heartbeat, but not many could say the same."

"Thanks for being sweet, Daddy," she says, releasing her grip on me long enough to pop up on her tiptoes to give him a kiss on the cheek. "Love you."

"Love you too," he whispers to her and gives me a nod.

He's not even two steps away when she hooks her arm with mine again and starts to haul me in another direction. If she made me close my eyes and find my way out, I'd be lost.

"I want to introduce you to my aunts."

There's no doubt in my mind we're heading toward a room filled with women. The talking is loud, and I hear a lot of laughter. But the moment we step into the room, there's nothing but quiet.

"I'd like you all to meet Nevin Walsh," Luna announces to the group, waving one hand in front of me.

I swallow, suddenly nervous and at a loss for what to do now. "Hey." I wave like an idiot.

"Those are my aunts Izzy, Angel, Max, Mia, Fran— watch out for her—and, of course, you know my mom." Each woman smiles as Luna says her name.

Mrs. Gallo is the first one up, and she's holding my nephew, Sal. "Nevin. It's been a long time." She pauses and covers her mouth. "Oh God. That came out totally wrong."

I smile. "No, Mrs. Gallo. It has been a long time. You haven't aged a bit either. Still as beautiful as ever."

"He knows how to sweet-talk," the oldest aunt says, pushing herself up from the table. "Let me get a good look at this man."

Luna leans over. "She's going to feel you up," she whispers.

"She what?" I ask, peering down at her.

"Just go with it. She's old and half out of her mind."

I turn my head as the old woman gets closer.

"Fran, leave the man alone. He doesn't want to be mauled," Mrs. Gallo tells her.

"The man has been in prison for ten years, surrounded by dirty, sweaty men. He could use a little love," the woman says, opening her arms to me. "Give me a hug, baby."

"Is she going to grab my ass?" I whisper to Luna.

"Probably," she tells me with a smirk.

"Oh boy," I mutter.

Before I have a chance to say anything else, Fran grabs me in a giant bear hug and damn near squeezes the life out of me. "He's so strong," she says, but she's the one who has me in a death grip with her thin arms.

"Fran, get your hands off that boy," Luna's grandmother says, stalking up behind the older woman. "I'm so sorry, Nevin."

I laugh, not hating it in the least. I've had worse shit done to me than a hug, with a small feel-up of my back, from an old lady.

"Why do you always have to kill my good time?" Fran asks as she releases me.

"He's a guest in our home."

Fran fluffs her hair as she shrugs. "And? What's your point, Mar?"

"He came for a meal, not a feel."

Luna snorts. "You two are insane. It's why I love you so much."

A shorter woman with long brown hair and killer high heels sticks her hand between the woman, extending it to me. "I'm Izzy, Luna's very protective aunt."

I take her hand, shaking it lightly and carefully. "It's nice to meet you, Izzy. I'm Nevin."

She stares at me. I feel the weight of her appraising gaze as she stares at me.

"Leave the boy be, Izzy. Please, make yourself comfortable, Nevin," one of the other aunts, the one with red hair, tells me. "Mom wouldn't want it any other way."

"Damn right," Luna's grandma says as she moves back toward the giant pot she was stirring when we walked in.

"Today is cavatelli and meatballs, plus a few other things."

My stomach grumbles. I have no idea what cavatelli is, but based on the smell, I'm guessing it'll be delicious. "Sounds fantastic."

"And by other things, she means a lot of things," Luna tells me.

"Do you eat like this every weekend?" I ask Luna.

She nods.

"Crazy," I whisper.

My lucky asshole brother hit the lottery hooking up with Rosie. I was wrong about her being uppity. She's been kind to me, when she really has no reason to be.

"You're part of the family now. You're welcome back anytime you want," Luna informs me.

"Really?" My voice cracks, I'm still so stunned.

I feel as if I've stepped inside a television show that's played on the oldies channel in black-and-white. I had no idea there were families who really acted this way. I haven't known any, and I sure as hell didn't meet anyone inside the joint who had this type of family experience.

"Really," the woman with long brown wavy hair tells me.

"Want to go outside?" Luna asks.

"Sure, Lu. Whatever you want."

She smiles up at me before looking around the kitchen. "Do you want any help?"

"No, baby," my grandmother says quickly. "We've got this. Spend time with your friends and cousins."

"Being a bad cook pays off sometimes," Luna whispers to me as we leave the kitchen and head toward the bank of sliding glass doors.

"Dinner will be in ten!" one of the women from the kitchen yells out.

"Got it!" a man from the other side of the house yells back.

I'm hit by a blast of hot air as we step outside onto the lanai.

"Hey," Rosie says, motioning toward the two empty chairs. "Come sit down."

I'm overwhelmed by the friendliness. Inside, life was rough. Rougher than I told anyone. There was rarely a kind word spoken to anyone or from anyone. If you showed any kindness, you were walked all over. I spent ten years convincing myself that I would never be weak and made being an asshole part of my personality.

"Hey," I say, collapsing into the patio chair with a fancy cushion.

"Beer?" Luna's cousin's husband asks.

"Sure," I tell him.

He reaches into a tiny fridge behind him, grabbing a few cold ones. He hands them out, and I'm half tempted to put the bottle against my face before drinking it. The heat and humidity have spiked today. Rare for this time of year.

"I'm Mammoth."

"Right. You own the auto shop, yeah?" I ask.

The guy nods before pushing back some of his hair that's fallen free from his ponytail. "I heard you used to dabble in custom paint work."

"Yeah. It's something I was learning before I went in. I'm obviously out of practice, and I'm sure things have changed."

"You'll pick it back up in no time. If you want to swing by the shop to practice, I'll always find time to help."

"For real?" I try to hold back my excitement. People always offer to help with things but never come through.

"Yeah, man. I'm always on the lookout for talent. Swing by one day and show me what you can do. Maybe we can work something out... That is, unless you want to stay at the bar."

"Hell no. I can't deal with drunk people all the time, and most tip like shit."

"He hauled a guy out of the bar the other night who was bothering me," Luna tells them, sounding like a proud parent. "I told him I had it under control, but like a typical man, he had to step in."

"As he should," Gigi says. "You don't need to fight all your battles, Lu."

"The guy was an asshole, but to be fair, Luna did break his finger before I helped him off his seat," I tell them, setting the record straight.

All eyes turn to Luna, and she smiles.

"You broke some guy's finger?" Tamara asks her.

Luna nods. "It was Oliver. He deserved it. I warned him first, but when he didn't listen, I did what I told him I'd do."

"I don't think I've ever..." Tamara's voice fades.

"My sis is pretty badass," Ro says, beaming at her twin. "But Nevin, I'm glad you were there to help her. Even if it was only Oliver. He's still a slimeball."

"Didn't need his help," Luna adds.

"I know you had it under control, but I couldn't sit back and watch him continue to be an asshole to you," I say.

"Damn, girl. Just say thank you," her cousin Lily says. "We all know you can take care of yourself."

Luna peers over at me. "Thank you," she says, but there's no enthusiasm in her voice.

"You're welcome," I tell her with a wink.

"I saw that," Tamara says, smirking.

Dylan opens the slider, finally making an appearance. "Dinner," he tells us.

"Does he always stay inside?" I ask Luna.

"Nah, but he's inside watching football with the guys. He and Dad bond during that time."

"He's such an ass-kisser," I say again, reaffirming what I've said before and witnessed too.

Luna laughs. "My dad loves having men around. Poor guy only had three girls, and we were not watching football with him. I swear, my dad kidnaps Dylan as soon as he walks through the door."

"Come on," Ro says, ticking her head toward the house. "They'll get pissed if we drag our feet. You know how the old folks get."

"I hope you're ready to eat, and when you're full, eat some more," Luna says to me.

"I've been prepping for a meal like this my entire life," I tell her, pushing back from the table and trying to remain calm. But I am as excited as a kid on Christmas morning, ready to dig in to all the homemade food.

I follow everyone inside, and Luna never leaves my side as we wait by the sliding doors for the line to move a little. "Fill up your plate," she tells me. "Leave no white space, or my grandma will be upset."

I peer down at her, soaking in her blue eyes. "I can't eat that much."

"Try. She would rather you leave food because you're too full than not eat enough."

"How the hell do you stay in such great shape?"

"I work out a lot and walk. Plus, I have great genes." She drops her voice to a whisper. "I've been trying to gain more weight because maybe my tits will grow."

I lean over until my face is buried in her hair and my lips are by her ear. "Babe, your tits are fantastic."

She pulls back, staring up at me and then back down at her chest. "They're kind of small."

"Anything more than a handful or a mouthful is a waste."

"Seriously?" she asks, looking down at them again. "They're just so...so..."

"Perfect. And if someone says anything otherwise, send them my way. I'll set their ass straight."

She glances away, suddenly interested in the food. "Oh, you're in for a treat. My gram made sausage and peppers to go along with everything else."

"It's that good?"

She places two of her fingers against her lips and makes a kissing sound. "The best."

"I'm ready." I rub my stomach, wishing I had left more room to eat.

"Did you think any more about my offer?" she asks as we finally take a step closer to the line of food dishes on the center island.

"Which offer?"

She steps in front of me, reaching for a dish. "Being roomies."

"Luna, I can't live with you."

"Why not?" she asks, her voice barely audible over the chatter of her family in front of us.

"I'll tell you later." I stare ahead, waiting for someone to turn around, but no one does.

"Tell me now," she demands.

I shake my head. "Later."

"You're not leaving here until you tell me."

"Fair enough."

She takes the biggest spoonful of sausage and peppers, dumping it on my plate. "Enough?"

I nod, knowing I'll never fit this all in my stomach.

"More?"

"No, Lu. I'm good."

She smiles, placing a portion a quarter of the size on her plate. That little amount of food isn't going to help her get bigger tits. If she thinks that, she has no idea how many calories are in everything.

By the time we make it to the other side of the kitchen, my entire plate is full, and the food is almost spilling over the sides.

"Inside or out?" she asks.

"Wherever you want. Where you go, I go."

And I wonder if I am still only talking about eating, or if I'd follow her anywhere.

Any friends I had before I went in are no longer around or don't want to associate with me anymore. Even with Ian's confession and my release, they still believe I was guilty or at least not good enough for them.

"Inside it is, big guy," she says, and I walk behind her, trying not to stare at her ass as she moves.

"They say it could make landfall later this week," her aunt with the red hair tells the table as we slide into two empty seats.

Thankfully, no one stops talking as we sit. I'm not the center of attention like a circus oddity anymore.

"They always move. I'm not worried," a man says.

She stares at him. "You never worry. It's why we're rarely prepared for when the shit really hits the fan."

He places his hand over hers. "Babe, I'm always prepared for everything."

Her stare doesn't waver. "Not for a hurricane, sweetie," she says, stabbing at the sausage on her plate with her free hand. "When you're eating chili out of a can, don't blame me."

He laughs. "We do have a grill."

"Can't grill when the wind and rain pound the house for twelve hours."

He shrugs. "I'll pick up a loaf of bread and some peanut butter. Happy?"

"Don't you have a stockpile of things from summer?" Luna's mom asks her.

The man and woman both turn their gazes toward Mrs. Gallo.

"You still stockpile every year?" the man asks her.

"The woman is always prepared," Joe tells them, but he smiles at his wife. "It makes her happy, and when she's happy…I'm happy."

"Is there a hurricane coming?" Luna finally asks.

"Yeah. You better prep," her mom tells her.

Luna sags in her seat and groans. "Why didn't you tell me earlier, Mom?"

"I didn't want you to worry," Mrs. Gallo replies.

"Since when?" Luna says with a snort.

"I know how scared of hurricanes you are, Lu."

"You're scared of them?" I ask Luna.

"I used to be petrified," she says. "But I don't worry about them much anymore."

"Since when?" her dad asks.

"Since I grew up," she says defiantly, raising her chin.

"If you say so, kid." Her dad smiles. "There're a lot of adults who fear them. Has nothing to do with age."

Luna goes back to her plate of food, stabbing at the shells of pasta. "Not me. Not anymore," she says confidently before shoving a huge forkful of pasta into her mouth.

"Whatever you say, sweetie."

I may not have known Luna for long, but I do know she's full of shit. She's putting on a show for her family. She hasn't outgrown her fear of the storms. If I were a betting man, I'd say it's as strong as ever.

LUNA

"The storm's expected to hit the Nature Coast on Wednesday. Currently, a Category 1, but she'll pick up steam in the Gulf's warm water," the reporter on the television says.

"Fuck," I mutter, trying to concentrate on the guy's tattoo.

"Looks like Sara is coming," Rosie says, strolling from the back to the front while staring up at the Weather Channel. "You want to come to our house?"

I shake my head. "No. I would rather stay at my place."

If I must be without electricity and ride out a hurricane, I'd rather do it alone in my own apartment. At least I can walk around naked and eat crackers. I don't want anyone else to see me have a panic attack every time debris slams against something, creating the most horrific noise.

"Seriously?" Gigi asks, kicked back in her chair with her feet up as she scrolls her social media feed. "Don't be alone. You'll freak out."

"I will not," I lie. "I'm not afraid anymore."

Rosie and Gigi both stare at me.

I hate that I'm so afraid of hurricanes. I've dealt with them my entire life, but I still can't get over the possibilities of what could happen. It's the only thing I'm truly fearful of in my life. I don't know if it's my stupidity and lack of self-preservation with most things, but I rarely get truly panicked.

"I'm not lying."

"Leave her be," Pike says, coming to my defense, which he often does when the two of them get on my case. "She said she wants to be alone. If she changes her mind, she knows where we live."

"Thank you, Pike," I say with a smile.

"What are you going to do if you have a panic attack in the middle of it?" Rosie asks while I shade the guy's giant eagle tattoo.

"I plan to be drunk or stoned the entire time. It's the only way to ride out a hurricane," I tell her.

Ro looks up, narrowing her eyes. "Is that smart?"

I shrug. "Sounds smart to me."

"I agree with her," the guy I'm tattooing says. "My cooler is going to be stocked. I plan to come out the other side without remembering a damn thing."

"Nice," Dylan mutters, staring down at his phone. "I don't see anything wrong with your plan, Lu."

"Everything is wrong with it," my twin sister argues with him.

I want to ask why Dylan is even here since he doesn't work at Inked, but I don't because he's on my side of this argument.

Dylan shakes his head, sliding a stool over toward Rosie's station. "Babe, leave her be. She'll worry about herself. She's grown."

She gives him a sour look. "Fine. What's your brother going to do? He can't stay at the Wayward Traveler. It's not safe. It's too close to the coast."

"I'll call him and see if he wants to come to our place, or if he's going to spend it with the rest of our brothers."

"Good." She leans over, kissing his cheek. "Thank you, but I'm not giving up on her."

I roll my eyes as I wipe the ink and blood off the guy's back so I can see what I'm doing. "Give up, Ro. I'm keeping my ass put at my place."

She groans. "So thickheaded."

"It's why you love me."

"Hardly," she mutters.

"Maybe someone should have everyone at their place."

"No way," Lily says. "I'm staying home with my family, curled up with a couple of good books."

"You think you're actually going to get any reading done?" Rocco asks her.

"I'm going to try, but knowing Jett, I won't get

many pages read. Anyway, it's a good time to reconnect as a family unit," Lily adds, earning herself a low murmur that lacks enthusiasm.

"I'm going to spend it curled up in bed with my woman. Maybe a little something more," Carmello says.

"You have another woman?" Arlo teases Carmello as she looks up from her laptop, working on her future novel she still hasn't published.

He smiles at her. "Babe. Come on."

Arlo points to her stomach. "You did this to me by curling up in bed. I'm going to be hot and sweaty when the power goes out. The last thing I'm going to want to do is have sex with you while I'm six months pregnant."

"I like hot and sweaty sex," he says with a wink.

She mutters a slew of obscenities while giving him the middle finger.

"Looks like you're going to read a book too," Lily tells Carmello, slapping him on the shoulder.

"Fucking great," Carmello says, shaking his head. "What if I buy a generator?"

Typical man. Always working an angle. He'd spend an easy grand on a generator just to get laid.

"There're none left. They sold out as soon as there were whispers of a hurricane heading this way," Lily reminds him.

"Damn it." Carmello scrubs his hands down his face as he relaxes back into his chair. "I should've been better prepared."

"Maybe next time, you will be," Arlo sasses.

"Nice," I say to Arlo, giving her an air high five, which she returns with a small giggle.

"Luna, can I have a break?" the man in front of me asks, stretching as I stop to dip my gun in ink.

"Yeah, Chuck. Ten good?"

"Yeah," he groans as he pushes himself up. "I'm too old to sit that long in one position."

"You're my last appointment of the day. Take your time."

He smiles, dipping his chin. "You're the best." He heads toward the front of the shop, leaving everything but his phone behind.

I grab my phone and notice three missed texts from Nevin.

Nevin: Sara's coming.

Nevin: Are you scared?

Nevin: What are you going to do?

I unlock my phone, going straight to the message app.

Me: I know. I'm not scared. I'll be fine at home. You?

Nevin: I haven't decided.

Me: Dylan's going to invite you over.

Nevin: Ugh. I would rather have my balls cut off.

I laugh as I read his text, understanding the sentiment perfectly.

Me: Why?

Nevin: I don't want to watch them make out the entire time.

Me: Truth. Are you going to your family's home?

Nevin: Rather eat glass.

Me: Why?

Nevin: Five men without showers in this heat? No way.

I stare at the screen, tapping my finger against the side.

Should I?

No.

I shouldn't.

But I want to.

If Ian were here, I'd be riding out the storm with him, laughing our asses off at my stupidity.

Shit.

Me: Do you want to come to my place?

Nevin: No, Lu. I'll be fine here.

I roll my eyes. I'm no longer the one with the hardest head.

Me: The Wayward is too close to the coast.

Nevin: I can swim.

"Impossible," I mutter.

Me: Don't be an idiot. You can keep me company.

Nevin: You need me to?

Me: I don't need it, but I wouldn't hate it.

I wouldn't hate it, but I wouldn't love it either. Lying around in my underwear under the influence of something is the only way I want to be.

Me: But beware. I don't plan on being sober.

Nevin: Do people go through hurricanes sober?

Me: Only the monsters.

Nevin: If it's coming, I'll be there on Wednesday.

Me: Good.

"Nevin's squared away for the storm," I tell Dylan and Ro.

"Good," Dylan says.

"Where's he going?" Rosie asks because she always needs more details.

"My place."

Rosie leans back, staring at me. "Is that a good idea?"

I stare back at her, letting my hands drop to my lap while still clutching my phone. "You'd rather I be alone?"

She closes her eyes and exhales. Got her. She can't say yes and feel like a good sister. "No, but…"

"Well, I won't be. You won't have to worry about me anymore." I smile at her, feeling smug as hell.

"You two should just come to our place," she insists.

I shake my head. "We'll have more fun at my place."

"That's what I'm worried about," she mutters.

"You're not my keeper, Ro. Nevin and I will be fine. We'll play Scrabble or something to pass the time."

She cocks her head to the side. "You don't even own a Scrabble game."

"Fine. We may get naked and dance around the living room. Happy?"

"Nothing wrong with that," Rebel says. "You're single and young."

"Babe, you're not old," I tell her. "Stop talking like you're Lily."

"Hey!" Lily yells from the front desk. "I heard that."

"Where's the lie?" I yell back before turning my attention back to my twin. "I promise to behave."

"Your promises are shit," she says. "Especially when you're intoxicated."

"Ro, live a little. I thought being with Dylan would make you relax a little bit, but wowee, I was wrong. Still as uptight as ever. You are certainly Mom's daughter."

She gives me the middle finger. "I'm relaxed and fun," she argues.

"Whatever you say, babe," I tell her.

"Just don't get knocked up," she warns me.

I point at my arm. "Birth control is firmly in place. I'm good for four more years. I'm not a moron. Plus, I'll be in survival mode. Remember the last hurricane?"

"I thought you were going to claw through the wall and hide between the studs." Rosie laughs. "You were insane."

"You think I'm really going to be looking to hook up with Nevin while I'm having a panic attack? I plan to stay as inebriated as possible, while staying alive."

Rosie shakes her head. "I just wish you were with me. You've never been without me for one."

I glance down, wondering if I can really ride out a hurricane without my twin sister, but knowing I have to try. "I'll be fine. We can't do everything together forever, Ro."

"I know," she says softly. "I hate it."

"Me too sometimes."

"If you need me, I'll find a way to get there, Lu."

"If I have to carry her on my back in the wind and rain, I'll do it," Dylan adds.

I laugh, picturing the absurdity in my head. "I may call just to see that."

"You have a few days to change your mind," Ro says.

"Give it up, sis," Gigi says, "She wants to be alone. She'll be fine."

"But she won't be alone. She'll be with Nevin."

"And?" Gigi replies.

Rosie shrugs. "They barely know each other."

"They'll know each other better after the storm. That much is for sure," Arlo adds.

"It'll give us time to talk about Ian. We have a lot of things to work through." It is a low blow, but I know by mentioning Ian, they'll leave me alone.

I have no plans to sleep with Nevin. He'll be my emotional support person through my first storm without my sister, and my apartment will be his safe haven.

I have no doubt we'll talk about Ian, and I'll do my best to fill in the blanks, letting Nevin know everything he missed. The least I can do is open my home to Nevin when he needs it most.

Chuck walks back in, having taken a little longer than I expected. "Ready?" I ask him as he settles back into the chair.

"I have two more hours left in me."

"I only need one," I tell him and immediately get to work.

When I'm done, I clean my station and head to the back room to restock for work tomorrow. Gigi and Rosie corner me.

"We're worried about you," Gigi says first, standing in front of Rosie.

"Don't worry," I tell them, setting down the blue ink bottle. "I'll be fine. We'll be fine."

"We're worried about you emotionally," Rosie says, changing course.

"I'm fine," I repeat, annoyed. "Jesus, it's not like Ian's dead." I place my hand on the counter, stopping myself from smacking them. "I'm going to say this one more time, and I need you two to hear me and hear everything I say."

They stand in silence, giving me their full attention.

"I'm fine. I'm not in emotional crisis. When I need another mother, I'll let you two know. But for now, please, for the love of all that's holy, let me live my own damn life."

Gigi lifts her hands. "Got it. I said what I needed to

say. You heard it. I heard you. We're done," she says and turns, leaving Ro and me.

"Don't you dare say anything else," I tell Ro as she's about to open her mouth.

She quickly snaps her lips closed and peels away from the doorway, heading the same direction as our elder sister.

"Fuck," I whisper as soon as they're gone. "They've all lost their damn minds."

15

LUNA

THE STORE IS CLEARED OUT BY THE TIME I MAKE IT there the next day. With Sara fast approaching, the people in the town have bought everything as if we are about to experience the apocalypse. The only thing I am able to grab is a giant bag of the lavender-scented Epsom salts that I love.

I stare at the freezer section where the pizza rolls used to be, stunned into silence. My bag at home is nearly empty, and now, there're none left to replenish my supply. At least I still have a case of ramen I ordered online last week.

A shadow passes by me and stops as I stand in the aisle. I ignore the looming figure and take a step toward the front of the store, ready to leave.

A hand lands on my upper arm, stopping my forward movement. "Luna," the man says as I tilt my head upward, catching sight of someone I haven't seen in months.

I instantly see red. If we weren't in the middle of a store, surrounded by many people who know me and my parents, I'd break his arm for laying hands on me, and then I'd kick him in the balls so he's never able to father children.

"Chad," I say, trying to keep the snideness out of my voice, but fail.

I hate this man. Hate may not be a strong enough word. If he'd spontaneously combust in the middle of the aisle, I'd spit on him and watch him burn.

Savage? Maybe.

But I've known too many Chads in my life, and none of them have deserved anything more.

He is worse than Oliver. Way worse.

He's vile and a tad on the unstable side. We went on one date. One that ended quickly and disastrously, but he felt the need to call me every day afterward for over a month. I always sent him to voice mail, and each message became increasingly hostile.

"Whatcha doing, baby?" he asks softly, like we're intimate and not strangers. "Are you stocking up for the storm?"

I feel my body stiffen as I remove my arm from his grasp and lift my chin, readying myself for whatever is about to happen. "I'm not your baby, Chad."

Chad is not fazed by the way I pulled my arm away from him. He's handsome. A deadly combination of crazy and pretty. But no amount of good looks will make me want to deal with him in any form. "I called you," he says like I didn't already know that.

"I know, Chad." I adjust the bag of Epsom salts, moving them in front of me to cover my chest, figuring if he tries anything, I'll throw the heavy weight right against his face. "I got all your messages, and although I didn't call you back, I figured you got my message loud and clear."

"I'm sorry about that. I was going through a rough time. I'm not normally like that." He moves his hand toward me like he's going to touch me, but I step backward, making sure it doesn't happen. "Will you give me another shot? We could be great together."

I shake my head, resisting the urge to smack him with the ten pounds of bath soak in my arms, although there's nothing I'd like more. In a town as small as ours, word will no doubt travel back to my parents or someone in the family. "Absolutely not."

"I think I deserve it," he says and does so with a straight face.

I jerk my head back, shocked by the man's audacity, but I quickly compose myself. I need to end this swiftly and make sure he has no doubt there's nothing between us and never will be either.

I lean in, getting closer to him, and drop my voice. "You don't deserve anything, especially my time. You had your shot, and you struck out. It's time to move on. And I'm warning you now, if you ever touch me again, you won't have that hand much longer to touch anyone else. Got me?"

Chad's eyes widen as his face reddens. "You can't mean that."

"Chad…news flash, buddy. When a woman says something, she always means it, and I'm no different."

He's absolutely the type of man who would think no means yes. He throws off the creep vibes like a tidal wave.

Chad brushes a hand through his sandy blond hair and blows out a breath, exasperated by the honesty I'm giving him. "Come on. Just a drink."

"No."

"A dinner?"

"No."

"Take you to a concert?"

I shake my head again. "Forget I exist, Chad. You're nothing to me, and I'm nothing to you. There will be no dinner, no date, no drink, no talk, and one hundred percent no calls. Leave me alone," I tell him, ending whatever fantasy he's already dreaming up in his head.

To an outside observer, I sound like a complete bitch. But a man like Chad needs a sharp tongue because any small amount of niceness will only allow him to believe that something more is possible when it's not.

"You'll change your mind," he calls out as I walk toward the front of the store with my head held high and my middle finger even higher in the air.

"Stupid motherfucker," I mutter under my breath.

I take my place in line, but as usual, the customer at the counter is asking a million questions, wasting everyone's time. On top of that, she pulls out her checkbook, and a collective groan goes up from the five people in front of me.

At this point, I'm beyond annoyed. I set my bath salts on the nearest endcap and head for the door, deciding bubbles will have to work their magic to save my sanity, my muscles be damned.

I stalk out of the store so pissed off, I'm not even paying attention to where I'm walking. When I hit something hard and bounce off, I start to stagger backward, knowing I'm about to ass-plant on the cement. Big hands grab my forearms, hauling me upward before I have the chance to bruise my tailbone.

"Luna?"

My belly does this weird flutter, a feeling I'm not used to and don't like in the least. My eyes drift upward to find his eyes trained on me as my hands grip his arm like he's the only thing keeping me tethered to the ground. "Shit. Sorry."

"Where are you rushing off to?" he asks without letting go of me. "What's wrong?"

"Nothing. Nowhere. I was just trying to buy a few supplies, but there's nothing left. I was just heading home."

"You were moving like you'd seen a ghost."

I snort, trying to play it off because the last thing I

need is someone to swoop in and try to save me. "Just saw someone I didn't want to see. You know how that is."

He releases my arms but doesn't move out of my way.

Shit.

Nevin isn't always about small talk, but today he seems extra chatty.

Yay, me.

"Did you get away?" he asks, studying my face.

"Well—" I glance behind me to see if Chad's following me out of the store too "—so far, yeah."

And like clockwork, Chad strolls out of the store, looking around the parking lot before his eyes land on me.

Fuck.

The man is relentless, and he's not only a mentally unstable creep, he's a persistent fucker too.

I do the only thing a sane woman would do in this situation. "Play along," I say to Nevin and throw myself against him, wrapping my arms around his neck and planting my lips on his.

Nevin's body stiffens, and at first, I'm kissing him but he's not reciprocating as quickly as I'd hoped.

"Please," I beg against his lips, and with that word, he slides his arms around my waist, and he presses his mouth against mine with such force, I think my lips may bruise.

Although the circumstances are forced, the act is

very real. His lips are soft, but the kiss is hard and demanding.

I melt into him, forgetting Chad's presence and not caring about anything other than tasting this man and feeling the hardness of his body against mine.

Every nerve ending in my body tingles, firing on all cylinders and wanting nothing more than to do this forever.

But reality sets in as Nevin pulls his lips away, gasping for air. He doesn't drop his hands, keeping them planted on my ass. "Shit," he whispers, breathing heavily and staring into my eyes with a look I can't quite decipher.

My head's spinning like I'm buzzing from too many drinks. "Sorry about that," I whisper back, keeping my arms locked around his shoulders, stroking the soft skin near his hairline. "I had to."

"You had to?" he asks, pinning me with those green eyes. "Why?"

"Shh," I say, not wanting to talk about Chad and wanting to bask in the memory of kissing Nevin. "Don't talk. Give me a minute."

Nevin chuckles deep, the vibrations coursing through my body and making the buzzing worse. "Finding your bearings?" He smirks, raising an eyebrow.

I grunt. "Based on the way you're breathing, I'd say you're the one trying to find your bearings, Nev."

His laughter only deepens. "You're a peculiar woman, Luna."

"Is he there?"

Nevin lifts his head, looking around the parking lot. "Is who there?"

"Tall blond guy in a white tank top."

He shakes his head. "The parking lot is empty."

"Thank fuck," I say, sagging against Nevin and finally feeling a moment of relief.

Chad's gone.

Hopefully for good. Maybe he saw the way Nevin and I kissed, knowing it's something he'll never have. If the man doesn't get the hint after today, he's dumber than I ever imagined possible.

Nevin's eyes darken, and his laughter vanishes completely, replaced by flat lips and a clenched jaw. "Who's bothering you?"

"No one anymore." I drop my hands from his shoulders but do so only because I know I have to. I could stay like this all day, kissing his perfect lips. "Thank you for playing along. I needed the save. I owe you one now."

"Babe, you owe me nothing," he tells me, peeling his hands and arms away from my body before putting a few feet between us. "We need to talk about this."

"No, we don't."

"Yeah, we do," Nevin argues.

"It was nothing."

"You came running out of the store like your ass was on fire. I'm not buying the *it was no one* shit."

I roll my eyes and shake my head. "He's seriously no one."

"You don't run that scared of anyone. Maybe other women do, but not you. The man has you rattled. Maybe you should tell your family about him. Maybe your uncles."

I shake my head, hating the idea of getting my uncles involved in something so stupid. "I have him handled and under control. I'm not getting my family involved in my business."

"The way you threw yourself at me, I'd say you don't have anything under control."

His words are like a punch to the gut and have me instantly on edge and ready to throw hands. "I did not throw myself at you."

"I'm not complaining, but if you're not going to tell someone about this man, I'll deal with him."

I square my shoulders and cross my arms. "I haven't seen the man in months. It was a fluke that I ran into him here. He's not stalking me. If I feel like he's after me and is a threat, I promise I'll go to them right away for help."

"Or me." He tilts his head, studying me. "You promise?"

"I promise," I lie. I'm not telling anyone shit.

If Chad does anything, I'll handle him myself. I've always handled things myself, preferring not to get my family involved, especially when it comes to my dating life.

"You want me to follow you home? Make sure the guy isn't there?"

"He doesn't know where I live. We had one disastrous drink together and nothing more. He's no one to me."

"He's someone enough to make you kiss me."

I roll my eyes. "Men," I mutter.

"I appreciate your help and offering to get me home safely, but I'm good. I've made it this long on my own, and I think I can do it again, but thank you for your help." I take a few steps backward toward my truck. "I'm good," I tell him, wanting nothing more than to get out of here. "Thanks, though."

Nevin rubs his hand back and forth through his dark-brown hair, which, in the sunlight, has flecks of gold. "If you need me, I'm just a phone call away."

"Got it. I'll see you Wednesday." I open my truck door and slide inside, happy to be alone and done with the interrogation.

I don't start the truck right away, continuing to talk to myself about my stupid decisions and how I always get myself into a jam, especially with men.

When I look up, ready to go, I spot Nevin. He's still standing in the same spot, arms crossed, shoulders wide, legs apart, and he's watching me.

I wave, plastering on a fake smile and shrugging,

because right now, I know I look like a lunatic by talking to myself.

He waves back, cracking a smile.

"I hate men," I whisper to myself, starting up the truck.

When I back out and pull away, I allow myself one last look in the rearview mirror, finding Nevin where I left him.

I know two things. One, I want to kiss Nevin again. And two, hunkering down during the hurricane may be the perfect time to make it happen.

16

NEVIN

THE WIND IS WHIPPING AROUND OUTSIDE, BUT THE apartment upstairs provides a buffer from most of the noise. The rain hasn't stopped in hours, and the worst of the storm is still coming.

"Do you think there's something after this?" Luna asks me as she lies sideways in a recliner, stoned and drunk.

She's softer than usual, her current state a clear side effect of the booze and the pot.

"I hope there is," I tell her, watching her from the couch across from her. "I really do."

She turns her head to look at me. "It's too awful to think of there being nothing."

"I know."

"Do you believe in God?" she asks me.

I should spare myself this conversation, but she's drunk and rambling. It doesn't matter because she isn't concentrating on the storm anymore, and that is important.

"No."

"No?"

I shake my head. "I don't believe there's some guy up by the pearly gates, waiting to judge me and either send me to heaven or hell. And if there is a God, he and I are going to have some serious words about the shit that happened in my life because that wasn't right."

She pushes herself up, or at least tries to, as her hand slips against the leather a few times. "Ian isn't a believer either."

I take another sip of my whiskey, trying to keep my buzz but not pass out. But my hurricane partner has no such worry, slamming back the booze like she's trying to win a drinking contest. "When you grow up like we did, it's not hard to understand why he doesn't believe. Do you...believe?"

She sighs. "I don't know. I want to. I was raised to, but fuck," she mutters, moving her head to rest her chin in her palm as her elbow rests against her knee. She struggles, barely able to find her own body for support. "It's hard to believe sometimes, but thinking the opposite is way too scary for me."

"You're scared that we only have this and then nothing?"

She nods and leans back. "This can't be all there is."

"But what if it is?"

"What's the point of it all if this is all there is?"

"You think there has to be a point?"

"Well, yeah. Duh."

"And if there's nothing afterward and no point to it all, would you do anything different?"

"No."

"Then what does it matter?" I ask her sincerely.

"Fuck if I know," she says, pushing herself up from the chair and placing her hand on the coffee table to catch her balance.

I watch her, thinking about reaching out to help her, but decide against it. Luna's capable, and the woman does not like to be treated like anything other than that. "Exactly, li'l moon."

"Li'l moon?" she says with a small laugh. "What's that?"

"You," I tell her, reaching out and brushing a few more locks of hair away from her face.

"Me?"

"Luna like moon, and you're tiny, hence li'l."

"I'm not tiny," she argues, which is part of her entire mood tonight.

"Tiny?" She then bursts into laughter. "I'm hardly tiny."

"You're smaller than me."

She lifts her arm, showing her palm to me. "Lemme see your hand."

I place my palm against hers as she studies the size difference. Her hand looks like it belongs to a miniature person instead of a full-grown woman when compared to mine. Her skin is soft and warm, a feeling I've missed.

Something smashes into the plywood covering the glass patio doors, and Luna jumps forward, half on my lap. She's shaking with her eyes wide.

"We're okay," I tell her in the softest tone possible as I wrap an arm around her.

She curls into me, burying her face against my chest. "I thought I could do this. I can't. I can't do this."

I cradle her head in my hand, holding her against me. "You can do this. I got you."

At this moment, she's not a tough woman who broke a man's finger. She's lost in her thoughts, petrified about something she can't control.

"I hate this," she murmurs into my T-shirt, clutching the material like her very life depends on the connection.

I lean back, bringing her with me. "You're safe."

"We have something like twelve more hours of this shit."

She needs sleep. It's the middle of the night, but neither of us has tried to lie down. The noise outside makes it damn near impossible at times to imagine dozing off. Hurricanes suck, but the nighttime storms are the absolute worst. They seem louder and more aggressive than anything during the day.

"Why don't you close your eyes?" I tell her.

She peers up at me but doesn't move any other part of her body. "Like this?"

I nod, smiling down at her beautiful face. "Yeah, babe."

She adjusts, lifting herself enough to bury her face in my neck. "I don't think I can sleep," she says.

But when her soft lips touch the skin near my jaw, any idea I had of sleeping flies right out the window.

"Luna," I whisper, not sure if I want her to stop.

She moans against my skin as she moves her hands down the front of my shirt, finding the bottom hem. When she slides her fingers underneath the material, making contact with my bare flesh, I nearly come undone.

It has been so long since anyone has touched me in this way. And far too long since I've had a woman in my arms.

"Luna, stop," I tell her, but I don't try to push her away.

She pulls her head back, staring up at me. "You don't want me?" There's a pout on her lips and hurt in her eyes. Hurt that I put there and never meant to.

"I do, Luna," I say, trying to control my breathing, which has become fast and harsh. "I just…"

"When was the last time someone touched you like this?" She pushes her hand farther up my shirt, scraping her nails against my skin.

I shudder, unable to stop the electrical current coursing through my entire body, making my cock's presence impossible to ignore. "Too long," I say, closing my eyes, basking in the sensation.

"I want you, Nevin. I want this," she whispers before her lips touch my neck again, and she adjusts her body until she's straddling my legs.

I glide my fingertips under the hem of her tank top, finding the softest, warmest skin I may have ever touched. I peer down as she looks up, and I grab her by the back of the neck, hauling her mouth toward mine.

She moans into my mouth, making me kiss her deeper, harder than before. The need becomes almost overwhelming, taking over my ability to think clearly or stop what's happening. She tangles her fingers in my hair, holding me to her as her breasts smash against my chest, drowning me in all things Luna. Her smell. Her taste. The feel of her weight against me.

Her tongue is silky, tasting of whiskey and sin. She takes control, kissing me harder, demanding more of me than I'd ever given to anyone else. I was only a punk-ass kid when I went to prison. My experience with women was limited at best. At this moment, I realize Luna's the more experienced. She's not a teenage girl who's unsure of how she wants to be touched.

"Wait," I murmur, pulling her mouth away from mine. "I haven't…"

Her eyes widen as realization dawns on her. "You've never?"

"I have once, Lu, but I was a kid, and I'm pretty damn sure it wasn't my best possible performance."

Her shiny lips turn up as her eyes soften. "There's no wrong way."

"You say that now." I stroke her back ever so slowly with my fingers.

"Nevin," she whispers, adjusting her middle against my dick, driving me a little closer to the edge. "Go slow and savor this. The only way we'll have an issue is if you jackhammer me into unconsciousness."

I laugh at the imagery. "I want to savor every moment."

The wind whips outside, lashing the tree branches against the covered window behind us. She jumps, but only clings to me tighter for protection.

"Make me forget," she murmurs, moving toward my lips. "Let me get lost."

I'm not sure if she's talking about forgetting about the storm or maybe something else. She's not giving herself to me out of pity or drunkenness. She wants to lose herself in me...with me.

"Make me feel good," she begs against my lips, staring at me with those haunting blue eyes.

I crush my mouth against hers, taking everything she's giving, wanting it and needing it just as much as she does. The kiss is unforgiving as my lips burn from the force. The sounds from outside are drowned out by our heavy breathing and moans.

I've never wanted anything more than I want this... want her. Moving my hand away from her head, I grab the hem of her tank, waiting for her okay. When she moves back, raising her arms, I lift the material from her skin. My heart hammers in my chest as I expose her breasts covered in black lace, looking every bit as full and beautiful as I've imagined.

And God, how I've imagined. No matter how many times I've told myself she's off-limits or a bad idea, I couldn't get the image of her naked out of my head. The idea of her dancing around in nothing but lace played on a loop as I stroked myself to completion every night while I was alone in my room.

"Fuckin' perfect," I whisper, trying to stop my voice from cracking like a prepubescent teenager.

She reaches behind her, looking me straight in the eye as she unhooks her bra. I watch with rapt attention, unable to stop myself from staring at her breasts as the material falls away, exposing her top half.

I swallow, salivating at the sheer sight of her natural beauty. "You sure?" I ask again, even though her taking the wheel and removing her bra leaves little doubt in my mind what she wants.

"Touch me," she whispers, reaching for my hand. Guiding my hand toward her body, she smiles softly and presses my palm to her velvety flesh.

I groan at the sensation, holding the weight of her breast in my hand and knowing I've missed out on so much for almost a decade. But if I hadn't gone away, hadn't done time for my brother, maybe I wouldn't be here at this moment with someone as free and special as Luna.

She slides her fingers down my abdomen, grabbing at my T-shirt, and I move, letting her lift it over my head. As soon as I'm free of it, I touch her breast again, wanting the connection.

She scoots forward, tipping back, thrusting her breasts closer to my face as if she's offering herself to me. I don't think twice as I bring my lips down on her soft skin while holding the other in my hand. My cock aches, begging me for relief, but I refuse to go fast and ruin the moment I've been waiting for since the day I was thrown behind bars.

As soon as you get your first boner, all you think about is sex. Being put away didn't diminish the thoughts or the frequency either. I had time to fantasize about a moment such as this, and that was the only thing that got me through each passing second, minute, hour, day, month, and year.

I pepper kisses against her skin, using my tongue to taste the saltiness of her flesh. I relish each lick and the way she responds, digging her nails into my flesh as she moans. She's absolutely stunning like this. Her long neck exposed, along with every inch of her top half. Her head tipped back, with her dirty-blond hair cascading down her back, lashing at my denim-covered thighs.

She spreads her legs apart, pulling mine with hers. "Touch me," she says again, and I know what she wants and that I can't say no.

She's wearing loose cotton shorts, baggy enough that she doesn't need to remove them. I slide my hand down her side, leaving her one breast without attention until I find the inside of her thigh.

I resist the urge to moan and call out to the gods for giving me such a sexual, confident creature who's begging for my touch as I glide my fingers toward her shorts. She's wearing nothing underneath, and my fingers find her warm core, covered in wetness from the way I've touched her.

She straightens her back, staring into my green eyes with her blue. "Be gentle. Worship me."

Am I falling for her?

Yes.

Do I love her?

Not yet, but I could.

I can feel myself falling. The hurricane known as Luna has me in her vortex, lifting me from the ground, unable to find my footing, and not giving a shit if there's an escape.

17

LUNA

EVERY INCH OF MY BODY SINGS, FEELING MORE ALIVE than I have in months, as Nevin settles underneath me. He has a look of wonder on his face as he stares up at me with his stormy green eyes.

I lean over him, settling my middle against his dick, as I take his lips and kiss him hard and rough. He moans as his hands find my thighs, holding on so tightly I may have a reminder tomorrow of where his hands have been.

His body stiffens below me as I slide my wet pussy against his dick, riding him like we're teenagers trying to avoid a pregnancy.

"Relax," I whisper against his lips. "I've got you. I just want you to enjoy this."

"Babe, I'm already enjoying this. There's no way I couldn't."

I reach to the side above his head, grabbing a

condom from my nightstand. I shimmy down his legs, getting a full view of his cock for the first time. It's beautiful. Straight as an arrow and so thick, the fullness will be sheer perfection.

He lifts his head and stares down his body at me as I rip open the wrapper with my teeth. His eyes never leave mine as I lean forward, placing the latex against his cock. It bobs, moving from the simple contact. I don't draw out the process, rolling the condom down his entire length.

There's nothing more to be said…only done. I crawl back up to his middle and lift myself up on my knees. I keep my eyes pinned on him as I grab his cock, watching the waves of ecstasy ripple through his system.

I rub the tip against me, wetting the condom to make this as easy for me as it will be for him. Slowly, I insert the tip, dropping my body at an excruciatingly slow pace. He tightens his fingers even more on my thighs as his body stills and his eyes squeeze shut.

"Breathe, baby," I whisper, easing myself onto his cock until he's fully inside.

"Wait," he begs before swallowing. "Give me a minute. Don't move."

I still my body, watching his face and the easiness that washes over him for the first time since I laid eyes on him. He's content and happy, something everyone deserves to be in their life.

I run my hands over his chest before bending at the

waist, wanting to kiss him again. He opens his mouth, welcoming my tongue and taste.

He drags me forward with his hands, and my clit rubs against him, sending a current through my body. I moan into his mouth, wanting him to know how very good he's making me feel.

This is slow and sensual. Something I haven't experienced with anyone else. Nevin's different. He's grown yet very much new and inexperienced. I'm aware of my prowess compared to his and how our feelings have been spinning out of control for weeks.

This is about more than sex. This is about a connection. Something we share that no one else can understand. It's a release for the feelings we've been bottling up with no means of escape.

I grip his shoulders, keeping my mouth sealed to his as I glide forward. His hands never leave my body as I ride him, slow and gentle at first. The feeling of his cock moving in me, stretching me wide, has my body on fire and my clit begging for the orgasm it's been missing.

No matter how badly I want to move fast, I don't. I ride him slowly in long strokes, drawing out everything as long as possible.

The windows rattle as the storm passes over us, but I don't care. The walls could come down around us, and I wouldn't get off him, taking everything I can from this beautifully flawed man.

It doesn't take long before he's pulling and pushing my thighs quicker, wanting and needing more than the torturous pace I've been setting. I give in, letting him control the speed, but grinding and moving the way I like. The way I know will tip me over the edge.

Within seconds, he's moaning, his body spasming underneath me. I'm not there yet, but something is missing. He lifts his hand, using his thumb on my clit, pulling me over with him. I scream out his name, milking his cock of every drop as the orgasm crashes over me, finally stealing my breath.

I collapse forward, plastering my body to his front with his cock still inside me. I pant, trying to fill my lungs with the oxygen they so badly need.

"Fuck," he mutters as he wraps an arm around my back.

"Bad?" I ask him, not bothering to look up.

He moves his fingers up and down my back, following my spine. "The fucking best."

"It was amazing," I say back, knowing my part was just above average. There was no extra spice or sizzle, but soft and sweet…something I'm not used to. "I'm so tired."

"Close your eyes, li'l moon. Sleep," he says softly, stroking my back even more gently.

I do as he says, closing my eyes and listening to the steady beat of his heart and feeling safe for the first time in a long time.

When I open my eyes again, the sunshine is sneaking through the cracks in the plywood. I scrunch my nose and squeeze my eyes shut again to block out the light. "Is it over?" I ask, feeling the unfamiliar warmth pressed against me.

"Yes. We made it."

"Thank fuck. Power still on?" I ask, praying that we're not thrown back into the Stone Age for God knows how long.

"Power never went out."

I relax into him, pressing my back as flat as I can against his front. "Did you sleep?"

"For a few minutes here and there."

"I slept like a baby," I told him.

He chuckles, tightening his arm around my waist. "I know. I heard."

I groan. "I do not snore."

"You do, and you talk in your sleep."

I roll onto my back, staring at him in disdain. "I do not snore, nor do I talk in my sleep."

He gives me a smug smile, tracing his finger across my collarbone as he holds his head up with the palm of his propped-up arm. "Yeah, you do, babe."

"What did I say, then?"

"You mumbled something about being happy. It was like you were talking to someone, but it wasn't me."

I close my eyes, remembering the most vivid parts of my dreams. "I saw Ian in my dream last night. That's weird, right?" I ask him. "Maybe he's trying to make us feel guilty."

"Babe, unless he teleported out of jail, I'd say it wasn't really him and he doesn't really give a shit."

"Don't be a smartass." I reach up, pinching his cheek. "Do you feel guilty?"

His eyebrows draw in, and he looks at me like I have three heads. "For what? Sleeping with you?"

"Well, yeah."

He laughs. "No, Lu. I don't feel an ounce of guilt or remorse about what happened. Quite the opposite. Do you feel guilty?" he asks me.

"No. Not really."

He smiles softly. "Not really means you do a little."

"Maybe a little."

"Why?"

"I feel guilty for being so happy when Ian isn't. You know?"

Nevin hauls me against his side as he rolls onto his back. "Babe, would Ian want you to feel guilty?"

I place my hand on Nevin's chest, nuzzling into his side. "No. He wouldn't want me to stop living."

"Do you love him?"

"I love him, but I am not in love with him. We don't have that type of relationship."

"What type is it, then?" he asks me, stroking my back again like he did last night.

"I never did this with him."

Ian and I had sex a handful of times. None of them involved cuddling or sleeping afterward. We went our separate ways or went for a drink afterward. We realized we were better off as friends and nothing else. Neither of us had the emotional capacity for anything beyond the physical.

"Did what?" Nevin asks.

"Snuggled."

"Never?"

"Never."

"I like that," Nevin says.

I look up, staring at his handsome face. "That makes you happy?"

He smiles. "Yeah. If that makes me a dick, I'm a dick, but I'm happy I had something with you he never has."

I close my eyes, still overcome with guilt and somehow content at the same time. "I don't think it makes you a dick."

"Good," he whispers, brushing his soft lips against my forehead. "I'd hate for you to hate me already."

"I don't think I could hate you, Nevin."

"Oh, I'm sure I could make you hate me if I really tried."

I smack his chest. "Don't you dare. I've had enough assholes in my life. I don't need another one."

Nevin laughs. "Don't get me wrong. I am an asshole, but I'll do my best not to be an asshole to you."

"Careful. I don't want to throw hands, but you've already seen me in action. I'm not scared."

Nevin laughs louder this time. "I might like to see that, li'l moon."

"Don't tempt me already," I mutter, snuggling into his side a little harder.

He holds me tighter, kissing the top of my head. "Should we get up and check out the damage?"

"No," I mumble against his skin. "I'm not ready to face the world."

"I don't have to be at work. Everything's closed. I can stay like this all day."

"The world can wait."

I close my eyes, following the dips and curves of his chest and abdomen with my fingertips until his breathing deepens, and I drift off again right behind him.

18

LUNA

THE BEDROOM DOOR CREAKS, AND THEN THERE'S A horrendous shriek. My eyes snap open, and I look down the bed, finding Rosie covering her face with her hands and staggering backward.

"What the fuck, Ro?" I ask, untangling myself from Nevin's body.

"Me?" she asks behind her palms as she turns around to face the wall. "What the fuck to you, Lu."

"This is my place," I remind her, pulling myself upward in the bed as Nevin yanks the comforter over his body to cover all his best bits. "What made you think you could just come in here without knocking or calling?"

"I lived here too, Lu."

"Lived," I snap as I grab my shirt off the chair next to my bed. "You can't walk into my bedroom anytime you want. We could've been in the middle of something."

She still has her face covered and has done nothing to move. "Looked like you were in the middle of something to me."

"In the middle of a nice fucking dream," Nevin mumbles as he lifts himself up and settles against the headboard.

"I called. We texted. No one heard from you, and we were worried. When I got here, I knocked. I banged. And nothing. I was fucking worried. I thought maybe you had a massive panic attack or something worse."

I climb to my feet and slide on the same pair of shorts from last night. "What could possibly be worse?"

"I don't know. Maybe you died from fear."

I roll my eyes at her dramatics. "Well, I'm alive and kicking, sis."

"And naked," she adds in a snarky tone.

"Not anymore, thanks to you."

"I am," Nevin says, rubbing his hands across his face as we both try to wake up.

"He's covered," I tell my sister, crossing my arms over my chest, so fucking pissed I'm seeing red. "You can turn around now."

Rosie turns, lifting her chin, looking like a prude. "I can't believe you two slept together."

And just like clockwork, Dylan fills the doorway. "Fuck," he hisses, zeroing in on his brother.

I narrow my eyes at my brother-in-law and my

sister. "You two had no problem when I slept with Ian, but now that it's Nevin, you suddenly have an issue?"

Their double standards are utter bullshit. I've never listened to anyone on how to live my life, and I'm not about to start now. Whether they approve of our friendship or the fact that we fucked each other, it is none of their fucking business.

"Ian was totally different," Ro says, making absolutely no sense.

Ian is the most emotionally unavailable person I know. He is worse than me, and that is saying something because I've run from anything resembling a relationship my entire life. Ian did so because of his cancer. He lived every day like it might be his last, and he only wanted happiness and fun, neither of which involved intimacy in his mind.

I place my hands on my hips, glaring at my sister and her absurdity. "That's the dumbest thing I've ever heard."

"Nevin, get your ass dressed. We need to talk," Dylan says, rubbing the back of his neck like the prick is about to stroke out.

"Got nothing to say," Nevin replies without moving. "Last time I checked, we're two consenting adults."

"Asshole." Dylan shakes his head, calmer than he was when he first walked in. "It's not like that. Please."

Nevin grunts and starts to get up, but the comforter falls, exposing his extra-beautiful cock.

Rosie squeaks, immediately turning around. "Oh my God," she wheezes. "I can't believe you'd do that."

"Sweet Jesus. It's just a penis," I tell her, groaning. "You see one every day."

"But it's *his* penis," she tells me, throwing a hand toward Nevin while closing her eyes.

Nevin pulls on his pair of jeans and stops next to me to kiss my cheek. "You two behave while we're gone."

I smile. "You too. Don't break any of my shit. Take your fists outside."

"No fists, li'l moon," he tells me with a wink.

"Li'l moon," my sister repeats and makes a gagging noise. "Gross."

I turn my glare back toward her. She's suddenly turned into my mother with her judgmental attitude, and I'm not having any of it. She needs to start acting like my sister and not my parents.

"Don't break any shit in here either," Nevin says, teasing me.

I tip my head toward the door and shoo him away. Nevin and Dylan stare at each other for a full thirty seconds in the doorway to my bedroom before they leave us alone.

"Stop being an asshole, Ro. You're not this person. You're usually the only one who never judges me, and I need that person now and not whoever walked through the door to my bedroom a few minutes ago."

She turns back around, arms crossed, head cocked. "I was so worried about you, thinking the worst possible things, and you're over here getting your brains banged out."

"Actually, I was banging his brains out," I say, trying to be funny, but she doesn't even crack the faintest smile.

She takes a deep breath before she speaks. "I'm being serious."

"Me too. There was nothing funny about what we did."

Nothing at all.

It was amazing.

Maybe everything was heightened because of the fear and panic coursing through my entire system as the storm raged outside, but it was unlike anything I've ever experienced before.

She takes a step toward me but stops a few feet away. "I just don't want you to get hurt."

"I'm not hurt. I'm the furthest thing from hurt. Why in the ever-loving hell would I get hurt?"

"I don't want you to regret this," she says, walking past me and sitting on the end of my bed. She fidgets with the chipped nail polish on her thumb. "This could easily end in disaster."

"You're not worried about him, and it could just as easily end in something amazing and special."

She peers up with no judgment on her face. "Maybe I'm the one who has a problem seeing you with someone else. I was used to Ian. I had dreams for you two. I made the plans. Saw what I thought your future would be, and nowhere in it was Nevin."

I sit down next to her, our shoulders touching. "Ian and I could never work. We were friends, Ro."

She turns her head toward me. "Friendship can lead to something more."

"Maybe sometimes, but not with us. Ian's a great friend, but he would be a shit boyfriend." I stare straight ahead at the open door. "I can only live my life the way that I'll be happy. I'm sorry you had dreams of us being more, but it's never going to happen, Ro."

"I know," she whispers. She reaches over, taking my hand in hers. "I don't think I've ever worried about you this much."

I squeeze her fingers, loving my sister even if she's a pain in the ass sometimes. "Stop worrying about me. If there were any other man in my bed, would you be scared or drag your ass over here, barging into my room?"

She shakes her head.

"You didn't think I'd make it through the storm without you, but I did, and that's only because Nevin was here."

"It's because you were doing the horizontal mambo."

"What are you? Ninety?"

She laughs.

"I hope Dylan isn't being a dick to Nevin," I say.

"I'll handle Dylan. Why don't you get dressed, and

we'll head to Grandma's place? They made food for everyone."

As much as I want to say no, I am freaking starving, and besides a couple stray pizza rolls and crackers, there isn't much in my cupboards or fridge. "Can Nevin come?"

"Of course."

I throw my arms around her, hugging her tightly. "You're my favorite sister. Do you know that?"

"I better be since you're my twin," she grumbles as she hugs me back. "God, you're such a pain in the ass sometimes."

"Takes one to know one," I tease her, but my sister is really too sweet. That's why I became more of a problem child. Someone had to stick up for her and make sure she didn't get eaten alive by the kids in school. "And Ro, don't ever barge into my bedroom again, 'kay?"

She pulls away, throwing up her hands. "Never again. I learned that one the hard way. Not something I plan to repeat."

"It wasn't hard."

She stares at me with her lips in a flat line. "You're such a jerk."

I elbow her in the side, trying to get her to laugh. "Just admit his dick is pretty."

"Penises aren't pretty, Lu."

"They're beautiful, Ro."

"I didn't look." She stands, ready to run out of my

bedroom like her ass is on fire.

"Liar," I tease, following her out of my bedroom to find the guys and hopefully not to play referee.

I fully expect to see Nevin and Dylan rolling around the living room, fighting like two dumb teenagers. Instead, they're sitting at the kitchen table, looking at their phones and drinking coffee like two old men.

"Are you two good?" Ro asks.

"Perfect," Dylan says.

I look at Nevin, studying his face. "Are you really good?"

He nods. "We said our piece."

Whatever they said to each other, it wasn't nearly as long or complicated as what Rosie and I said in my bedroom. But as with most men, that's not entirely surprising.

"My grandparents are having everyone over," I tell Nevin. "You want to come?"

Nevin's gaze moves from me to my sister and then to his brother. "Should I?"

"Come," my sister says. "They're expecting you."

"Oh boy," Nevin mumbles. "Does everyone know I spent the night?"

"I don't know if they know, but I can guarantee the news will spread like wildfire before we get there," I tell him as I reach for a coffee mug.

"Everyone knows how Lu is with hurricanes."

"She wasn't bad at all," Nevin tells Ro.

I fill my mug, ignoring them as they talk about me

like I'm not in the room. All I care about is caffeine and my small hangover.

"Someone kept my mind on other things," I say with my back to them, smiling against the rim of my mug.

"I don't want to hear details," Rosie replies immediately.

"It wasn't like that. We talked most of the night," Nevin tells her.

"But not *all* of the night," I add, turning back around to face them.

My sister touches Dylan's shoulder. "Why don't we head over, and they can meet us there when they're ready."

Dylan rises from his chair, coffee cup in one hand, and grabs my sister's other hand as it drops from his shoulder. "Whatever you want," he says to her.

"I think they need more time to wake up, even though it's one in the afternoon."

"You know I like my sleep," I remind her.

"I can't forget."

"How are the roads? Any storm damage?" Nevin asks Dylan.

"Nothing you can't work around in Luna's truck," Dylan tells him.

"We'll be there in a bit," I say to my sister as she makes her way toward the door. "Don't go off the rails and tell everyone what you saw."

"I won't tell anyone you two were in bed," she promises.

"I mean about his beautiful penis," I tease my sister, earning an eye roll in response. "No one needs to be jealous."

Dylan grunts. "You guys don't talk about our dicks all the time, do you?"

I smile. "Oh no. Never," I lie.

We know everything about everyone. Who's pierced. Who's not. Who has a curve. Who's straight as an arrow. I won't talk or listen to anything about people I'm blood-related to, but the men who weren't born into this family…I know everything about them.

Ro stops at the door and turns back toward the kitchen, where I'm still nursing my mug of coffee. "Don't take too long. Dad's on edge today."

"Fuck," I mutter.

"Maybe I should head home," Nevin says.

"Oh no." I grab on to his shoulder, keeping his ass in the seat. "You're coming with me. I may need protection."

He peers up at me, narrowing his eyes. "Who's going to protect me?"

"I got your back if you got mine."

"Doesn't seem fair. He isn't going to kill his own child."

"He's not going to kill you either."

"Liar," Nevin barks out.

My stomach turns, thinking about my dad. There's only one thing scarier than Mother Nature, and it's a pissed-off Joseph Gallo.

19

NEVIN

"Honey, come here," the old woman who felt me up the first time I came here says, patting the chair next to her. "I want to talk."

I stay where I am, holding the plate of food and looking very much like a deer in headlights.

"Promise," she says again.

"Go see Fran. She's harmless, but watch out for Bear."

"Bear?" I ask, peering down at Luna as she stands next to me with half as much food.

"Her husband. Big, bulky biker, looking like an ancient Santa Claus."

"You sure?"

"She only does that to get a rise out of her man. He's the jealous type, and she likes what jealousy does to him."

"What's it do to him?" I swallow, hoping I didn't

survive prison and a hurricane only to be taken out by an old Santa.

"I've never asked because I don't want to know."

I crack a smile. "I don't want to know either."

Luna dips her chin toward the old woman who's sitting at the table in the kitchen. "Want me to come with you?"

"Yes," I snap. "Of course I do. Don't throw me to the wolves."

She giggles. "Fran is hardly a wolf."

I blink and narrow my eyes. "Are you blind?"

She laughs again. "Come on, big baby," she says, moving toward the otherwise empty table.

"Hey, Auntie. How did you two do during the storm? Any damage?" Luna asks her great-aunt as I slide into my seat.

Fran stabs at a small piece of lasagna. "Not much damage at all. Bear had it all cleaned up before we headed over here. How about you, sweetie? You have any damage?" she asks, waggling her eyebrows.

"Nothing of note," Luna tells her. "But that's apartment life."

"I heard you weren't alone." Fran looks at me and smirks. "I hope you two were able to sleep with all that ruckus."

"We didn't sleep much. It was a hell of a storm," Luna tells her, pushing the food around on her plate.

"I'm sure that's why you didn't sleep." Fran pats my hand and doesn't wipe the smirk off her face. "I'm sure it has nothing to do with this fine young man next to me."

"Fran," Luna warns. "Get your mind out of the gutter."

"I'm old and hunched over. It's the only place my mind goes these days, Lu… Thank God."

Luna looks around. "It was a very innocent evening."

"I'm disappointed."

"Why?" Luna asks her.

"You're only young once, Lu. Don't waste a minute of it trying to be proper. Because when you get old like me, you'll realize you wasted your youth being boring as hell."

I smile at the old woman, loving her outlook on life.

"And this one's already lost enough years. He doesn't need to be sitting around bingeing television or playing chess."

"Chess?" I ask her, almost choking on my lasagna. "I don't play chess."

"It's a metaphor, child. I see the spark between you two. It burns bright, and I'm figurin' it has something to do with what happened last night while you were there trying to keep her ass calm."

"Nothing happened," Luna lies.

Fran lifts her fork, pointing it at Luna's chest. "That hickey on your neck says otherwise."

Luna gasps and tries to cover the spot her great-aunt

just pointed to. "What the hell, Nevin? Are you sixteen?"

I stare at her, seeing absolutely nothing and remembering last night very clearly. "Babe, I didn't mark you."

"Got ya," Fran says, laughing until she snorts. "Can't lie now."

"Damn it," Luna mutters, dropping her hand back to her fork. "I can't believe I fell for that."

"It was way too easy," Fran tells her, still laughing.

"What was easy?" asks a man who does, indeed, look like an ancient Santa.

"Nothing, baby," Fran says to him. "Just talking to the kids about the storm."

"Hell of a night," he says. "I'm exhausted after picking up that damn yard. I think it's time for a condo."

Fran's eyes widen. "Throwing in the towel, old man?"

"When it comes to trees and grass, fuck yeah. You going to do it when I'm too old to walk?"

She shakes her head. "I can't do it now."

"Condo, Fran. Condo with a pool."

"We'll start looking this week," she tells him, reaching over to rub his beard. "I'm ready for a change."

"As long as you're not trading me in," he says while kissing her cheek.

"Not on your life," she says with a smile.

"I ain't letting you go so easy, Fran."

"I'm going to jump in your grave when you die," she tells him.

I watch their conversation in weird fascination. They love each other, but it's not the stuff they show in the bullshit Hollywood movies. It's clunky and awkward, but it's plain as day.

"How are you doing since getting out?" he asks me right as I'm shoving a big helping of lasagna into my mouth.

Since my mouth is full, Luna answers for me. "He's working at the bar and staying at the Wayward."

Bear grimaces. "Trash place. Always has been. Always will be. They still have mirrors on the ceiling?"

I shake my head, hating that I can't reply to him, but chewing the flaming-hot lasagna as quickly as possible.

"It isn't as bad as I thought it would be there," Luna tells her uncle. "I asked him to move in with me, but…"

"Your father would shit a brick," Bear tells her flat out, which isn't a lie.

Joe Gallo may be okay with me hanging out with members of his family, but becoming the roommate of his last single daughter… That would be a hell no.

"I don't need his permission, Uncle."

The lasagna almost lodges in my throat when she says that. She's a little rebel and I love that about her, but damn, the last thing I need is more trouble.

I pound on my chest until I get the food to pass through my throat. "It's for the best that I stay at the Wayward."

"Smart kid," Bear mumbles, lifting his fork in my direction. "City don't play when it comes to his girls."

"I'm sure the prison thing doesn't help either," I tell him.

He shakes his head, and even though his mouth is full, it doesn't stop him from replying. "I've been behind bars more times than I can count, and City's always been there for me. Never judged. Hell, that fucker's had his fingerprints taken a few times too."

"What?" Luna gasps. "When?"

"It's been a few decades, but he never shied away from getting his hands dirty, but only when helping a friend."

"Dad? I still can't believe it." Luna shakes her head softly. "He's so…"

"Your dad was badass in his younger days."

"I still am, asshole," Mr. Gallo says, sitting down in an empty seat next to Bear. "You're the one who's gone soft."

"We're both soft. We're not young bucks anymore." Bear laughs, slapping Joe on the back. "But trouble still finds me, while you're at home knitting sweaters."

Joe gives him a look of death, the same look he used to give me and my jackass brothers when we were young. "I've just gotten smarter, while you continue to get caught. You haven't learned a damn thing over the years."

"Sometimes I want to get caught," Bear tells him

while shoveling in another forkful of lasagna. "It's like a vacation."

"It sure is a vacation for me," Fran adds, giving Luna a wink.

"I still can't imagine my dad getting arrested," Luna says, staring at her father like the man walks on water.

"You should've seen him before he met your mother. The man was a lunatic."

Joe glares at Bear, and I swear to God, the air in the room damn near evaporates. "Don't put shit in my kid's head."

Bear sets his fork down, staring back at his friend. "What shit?"

"I don't want her thinking all criminals are good guys," Joe says.

My stomach knots, but I keep eating, knowing damn well he's talking about me. No matter what he says, I still served ten years in prison. A person never comes out the same way as they went in, even if they're innocent.

"I don't think that, Dad. I know the difference between a good person and a bad one, no matter where they've been."

"Even the best-dressed businessman can be the most evil person. Can't always judge someone by how they look or the shit they've been through in life. Right, kid?" Bear says, pausing and waiting for a reply.

I look up from my plate, finding him staring at me and not Luna. "Me?"

"Yeah, dum-dum. I'm sure you met all kinds when you were inside. They don't all come in looking like they're the big bad wolf when they're the worst of them all."

"Yeah. Plenty," I mutter.

Bear leans back, studying me as he rubs his gray beard. "You know we're not talking about you, right?"

"Sure," I mutter.

Bear doesn't stop staring at me. "Kid, you did a good thing. I don't care how long you sat behind bars, you did good. I've done some pretty shitty things in my day, but I never went to prison, and I wouldn't have gone to prison for something I didn't do."

I set my fork down, suddenly losing my appetite. "I didn't have a choice."

"Everyone has a choice," Joe replies. "You didn't have to confess to a crime you didn't commit. Ian didn't make you. As far as I know, he didn't ask you to either."

"He didn't." I fidget with the napkin in my lap.

"Then you had a choice, and you did it because you loved him. When we talk about bad people and criminals, we're not talking about you."

I sigh. "It's hard to think of myself as anything but. I had ten years when I was treated like the worst type of trash, and then the years before that when my father treated me and my brothers the same way. It's hard to think of myself as good."

"Get the fuck over yourself," Joe says. "You are good. End of story. I may not have liked you much as a kid, because let's face it, you were all dicks, but I respect you as a man."

I sit back, humbled that a man such as Joe Gallo respects me. Never thought that would happen in my lifetime, and I sure as hell didn't think I'd hear the words uttered from his very lips.

Luna grabs my hand under the table and squeezes. "He's one of the good ones."

"Don't find men like that very often," Aunt Fran says.

"We're only friends," I say quickly.

Luna's hand disappears. "Right. Friends," she whispers as her shoulders slouch forward.

Well, I fucked that up and did it big in front of her father. Way to go, moron. Although I'm in my midtwenties, I still have only a handful of years of experience with women and relationships. And what the hell did I know when I was sentenced and hauled off right after my eighteenth birthday? Not a goddamn thing.

"With benefits," Fran coughs into her napkin.

"What are you talking about in here?" Rosie asks, walking into the kitchen with an empty plate.

"Dad's jail time," Luna says, waving a hand at her father. "He's been arrested a lot. Like a lot, a lot."

Rosie drops her plate to the counter and spins around. "He what?"

Luna nods. "Yep. Has a record a mile long. Uncle Bear too."

Bear laughs. "Come on. Almost everyone here has

been arrested. Hell, even your grandfather."

Rosie covers her mouth, wide-eyed. "I can't…"

"Shut the fuck up, Bear," Joe grumbles, scrubbing his hand across his face. "Let the kids live a fairy tale."

"Oh no," Rosie says, stalking toward the table. "I want to hear this. What did Grandpa do?"

Joe shrugs. "Have to ask him."

"And you?" Rosie asks her father.

"Which time?" Bear says, laughing again and not giving two fucks how Joe feels.

"Oh my God. For real?" Rosie whispers.

"Don't listen to him. He's an old man with a bad memory," Joe tells Rosie.

"Bad memory?" Bear places his elbows on the table and sports a shit-eating grin. "I clearly remember when you and your bride were arrested, and I had to post bail because you were—"

"What?" Rosie screeches.

Luna covers her ears. "I don't want to hear this."

"That's enough, baby," Fran says to her husband. "You've scarred them enough for one day."

"Think of it as a bonding experience," he tells her.

She shakes her head. "You're rotten to the core."

"Just how you like me, sweetheart." He leans over, kissing her on the cheek. "Now, finish eating because I have a bed that's calling my name, and I want you in it with me."

I smile, feeling awkward as hell, but I like these people. Each one of them is good and loves the others.

Being around the Gallos, I realize how much I was robbed of as a kid. We had no family around, and the little bit we did have wanted nothing to do with my father or us after Mom took off. I can't blame them. My father was a shitty human, but we were innocent, caught in the cross hairs of our age.

"You want to go outside?" Luna asks me. "I'm sure they're chomping at the bit to talk to us."

"Sure," I say, but I don't mean it. I'm comfortable around the older people...even Joe Gallo, and that's saying something.

The last thing I want to do is answer more questions and fuck up. I already inserted my foot into my mouth with the "friends" comment. I'm sure I'll end up digging my hole even deeper once I'm around her cousins. I might as well throw myself in it and cover myself with dirt.

"Leave your plates. I'll get them," Fran says, motioning for us not to touch anything.

"Finally," Rosie says to Luna as we get up. "There's lots to discuss."

"There's nothing to talk about," Luna tells her.

Yep. I'm dead. I went from winner to in the doghouse in the matter of one word. I wish I could go back and not open my big fat mouth, but shit doesn't work that way.

We haven't talked about what we are or aren't, and in a moment of panic, I said the wrong thing.

Fuck!

20

LUNA

"Why do you need me here?" I ask Trace as he opens the door to ALFA Security, waiting for me to walk in first.

"Moral support."

I stop before I have both feet inside the office and turn my head to stare him straight in the eye. "Moral support for…"

Trace smirks, and I immediately know whatever he's about to drop on his dad isn't going to be something Uncle James will be happy about. "I may have gotten myself into a jam."

I raise my eyebrows, wanting to know more. "A jam? What did you do? Steal a car? Rob a bank?" I giggle at the absurdity.

Trace has always been the wildest one of the younger boys. His older brothers, Carmello and Rocco, had their share of crazy, but Trace has always worked extra to get attention. He is a kindred spirit to me since I am the youngest out of my siblings too.

Trace doesn't laugh with me, though.

"Holy shit. You stole a car?"

"No," he replies, wincing. "But this may be worse."

"Damn." I shake my head, trying to hold back my laugh. He's going to get his ass chewed out by my uncle big-time. I know it, and Trace knows it too. "Based on your dad's connections, I'd say there's a good chance he already knows. Hiding anything from our fathers is damn near impossible in a small town like this."

"He would've said something if he knew, and since he's been radio silent, he knows nothing."

"Mind games. They all play them too," I say.

Trace shakes his head as he pushes me inside. "He's not playing any…yet. But I have a feeling he's going to find out today, and I'd rather be the one to tell him. I plan to beg for mercy, forgiveness, and his help."

"Dumbass," I whisper before plastering a smile on my face as Aunt Angel sees us and begins to stand.

"Luna. Trace," she says, grinning softly and rounding her desk to meet us in the reception area. "And to what do we owe this honor?"

I pitch a thumb over my shoulder. "Trace wanted to talk to his dad."

Aunt Angel wraps her arms around me and whispers, "What did he do?"

"Don't know, but I'm sure there will be fireworks," I whisper back as we hug.

"Sweet Jesus," she mutters, but she doesn't miss a step or let her smile falter as she steps back and moves in to hug my cousin.

"It's not that bad, Auntie. I promise," he says, but he doesn't look her in the eye when he talks, which instantly sets off alarm bells.

"Would you rather talk to Tommy?" Angel asks him.

I chuckle softly because Uncle Tommy is just as scary as Uncle James when he's mad. I always thought my dad was the scariest of all his brothers, but I learned that was a lie as I grew older.

Trace shakes his head. "No, Auntie. My dad needs to know what's going on. I've waited long enough to tell him, and I could really use his help and advice."

Aunt Angel strokes her long red hair, smoothing it over her shoulder. An instant tell that she's about to drop a lie. "I'm sure everything will be fine, no matter what you're about to tell him. Your dad can be a very under-standing man."

"Sure. He's the pinnacle of calm and patience," Trace says with a snort. "I've lived a nice life. If it ends today, at least I know I lived it to the fullest."

I slap Trace square in the chest with the back of my hand, and Trace flinches, but the impact isn't enough to make his body move. "Stop being a drama queen. The man isn't going to end your life because you did some-thing stupid. I'm sure he's seen his fair share between Carmello and Rocco."

"Those boys were always getting into some type of

trouble. All three of you and Nick remind me so much of your dad and Tommy when they were young. They were practically feral." Aunt Angel grabs Trace's hand, taking his attention away from his father's closed office door. "It'll be fine. I promise," she says to him. "You can go in. He's finishing up with a new client."

"Thanks, Auntie," Trace says, giving Aunt Angel a warm smile. It's hard not to be sweet to her and believe everything she says, especially when she's lying.

"Come with me," Trace begs me. "Walk in with me and say hi. Then you can leave."

"Good because I'd rather not stick around to watch your death. Do you want to be buried or cremated?" I ask, feeding into his panic that's brewing right under the surface, barely visible.

"I'll be dead. What the hell will I care?"

"This is going to be an interesting afternoon," Aunt Angel mutters as she saunters back to her desk to answer the phone. "ALFA Security. This is Angel. How may I help you?"

"You go first," he tells me, pushing me toward the hallway to his father's office.

"Pussy," I whisper under my breath as I take a few steps forward. "I'm not scared."

"Because you didn't do anything wrong, and he's not your father."

"I've done plenty wrong, but I've never done something dumb enough to need my dad's help."

"There's still time," he says to me as he follows close behind me.

"Don't be ridiculous. I tend to think through things before I get my ass into too much trouble."

"Lu, you're all about impulse. You don't think about shit but boys and dicks."

"Men," I correct him. "Men and dicks. Both of which cause nothing but trouble, but I never break the law."

"Never say never."

I grunt, stopping outside his father's office door. "You ready? I'm giving him a hug, and then I'm leaving you to fend for yourself."

"Your appearance will soften him a bit in case he's having a shit day."

I laugh. "I'm sure my face will lessen whatever is about to be unleashed."

"It will. Don't go far, because if you leave me…"

"I'm not going anywhere, Trace. I'll go in and soften him up, but then you're on your own. I'll wait out by Aunt Angel. Ready?"

He hesitates and is about to chicken out. So, I do the thing he needs me to do and knock. "Uncle James," I call through the door. "Can I come in?"

"Luna?" he says before the sound of loud footsteps fills the air.

Trace's body stiffens, and his face drains of color.

Man, whatever he did must be big and bad. I'm going to have to twist his arm and force him to spill all the details when we get in the car to head back to Inked. There's no way I'm going to play offense for him and not find out what I'm putting my neck on the line for.

The door opens, and Uncle James greets me with a big smile. "Hey, kid," he says, his voice deep but gentle. "It's nice to see you here." But just as those words leave his mouth, his gaze lands on Trace, and his easy smile evaporates. "Son."

"Hey, Dad," Trace says, waving his hand like an idiot.

"What happened?" Uncle James asks because he's not a moron like his youngest son.

When Trace doesn't answer, I feel the need to jump in and take some of the heat off him. "I don't know what he did, but I wanted to stop by and say hi. I couldn't come here and not say hello to my favorite uncle."

"My brother-in-law is a lucky bastard to have three sweet girls," Uncle James replies.

"Bullshit," Trace coughs, earning himself a raised eyebrow and a stare that would've had me piss myself as a kid.

Uncle James is easily over six feet tall with wide shoulders. When I was little, I thought he was big enough to block out the sun. I never understood how Aunt Izzy, who is nowhere near his size, could handle this man and do it with ease. I looked up to her and how she could use her smarts and sass to make such an imposing man do just about anything she wanted with a few words and flicks of her eyelashes.

We peer inside and see there's a man sitting in a chair across from Uncle James's desk.

"We don't want to interrupt," I tell him, keeping my gaze locked on the back of the stranger's head. "You have a client."

"We'll come back, Dad," Trace says, chickening out.

I don't blame him for chickening out. I'd chicken out too if I had to tell Uncle James something I knew would make him mad. I hated telling my father anything stupid I did, and the man was pretty damn easy. Having three girls, he knew we could turn on the waterworks in an instant, and the big guy never did well when tears were involved.

"I think we're done here," the stranger says, standing from his chair, and as soon as he turns around, my blood runs cold.

Uncle James turns to face the man. "I'm sorry. We'll only be a few minutes if you'd like to wait in the reception area. Angel can get you a coffee."

"Chad," I whisper, narrowing my eyes and envisioning his death at my hands.

"It's not a problem, Mr. Caldo. I may not need your services after all. I may have just found the lead I needed," Chad tells him, smiling at me.

"Luna." Trace elbows me in the ribs. "What's wrong?"

I'm barely breathing at this point. "I'm fine," I lie,

wanting to keep my business away from my family. "It's nothing."

Trace leans over and drops his voice so only we can hear. "You're white as a ghost. I'm the one supposed to panic, not you. Remember?"

"I know him," I whisper.

"You know him?" Trace asks, his head turning toward the guy walking in our direction. "How?"

"Not important," I say as Chad slides by me, keeping his gaze pinned on me.

"Who is he?" Trace asks me when Chad is a few feet away.

"A dead man," I tell him, waiting for him to walk out the front door before I excuse myself. "I have to run. I'll catch you later, little cousin."

"Wait. We need to talk," he says to me, grabbing my arm before I can walk out of Uncle James's office.

"You worry about you. I've got this. I'm not a shrinking violet."

"What?" He gawks at me, clearly never having heard the phrase before.

"Nothing." I pat his shoulder. "Keep your ass alive."

"You too," he says with a sad smile.

The door is halfway closed when Uncle James yells my name.

"Fuck," I hiss and stop. "Yeah?" I turn, plastering a fake smile on my face.

He motions for me to come in. "Stay."

"But I have…"

He gives me a look, and I know it well, having seen it on my father's face more than once in my lifetime.

"Fine," I grumble and step inside his office, closing the door behind me. "I don't think—"

"Sit," Uncle James commands, and my ass drops into the chair without any argument.

He studies me for a minute, leaning back in his chair with one hand rubbing his chin. It's unnerving. "What was that?" he asked me.

"What was what?" I shoot back, playing stupid.

He ticks his chin toward the door. "That."

"I was just going to run home."

His eyes narrow. "Don't play coy. You knew that man."

I sag forward, hating this. "Met him a few times. He's an asshole."

"As soon as your eyes landed on him, everything about you changed. I need you to be a little more forthcoming about him and how you know him."

I sigh and lean over my knees, staring at the floor. "Can I handle it, please? I don't want to get anyone else involved in my problems. You have enough to handle with Trace and his dumbass shit."

"I'll handle my dumbass son in a moment, but right now, I want to talk about Mr. Downs and why your entire demeanor changed when you saw him."

"Tell him," Trace says.

I turn my head and glare at my cousin. "You just

want to prolong the delay before your ass gets chewed out."

"Eh," he mutters, waving a hand. "I'm a dead man either way. Sooner or later. Doesn't matter. But something ain't right, cousin. You're always fearless, and from what I just witnessed, that light switch flipped in an instant."

I sit up straighter, readying myself for what I'm about to tell my uncle and knowing the consequences will be completely out of my hands. "I know Chad."

"How?" Uncle James asks.

"We went on a date."

"And what happened?"

"He wasn't my type. He gave me the creeps, and I ditched him. Clearly, I wasn't wrong about the guy because he's a major tool."

James leans forward, placing his hands on the desk. "What did he do?"

"Well…" I inhale and close my eyes, wishing I'd never agreed to come with my dumbass cousin. "Do I have to tell you?"

Uncle James stares at me and reaches over and grabs the phone. "Can you come in here, please?" he says to someone.

"I don't want anyone else involved," I beg.

"Too late," he says, not giving a single fuck about how I feel or what I want.

The door to Uncle James's office opens and closes, and I don't turn around. I'm too scared to even move.

"What's up?"

I squeeze my eyes shut as soon as I recognize the voice.

"What happened?" Uncle Thomas asks.

James turns his chair to the left and then to the right, pointing a finger directly at me. "Had a client in here, and he wasn't throwing the right vibes. Luna showed up, and the color drained from her face when she laid eyes on him."

"What he'd do?" Uncle Thomas asks, moving toward Uncle James's desk. He sits on the edge, staring at me too.

Fucking great.

"He hasn't done anything yet. Not really."

Thomas folds his arms over his chest. "And what's not really mean? Has he laid hands on you?"

I shrug. "Kind of, but not really."

Both of their bodies straighten and still.

"Explain," Thomas says. "You're not in trouble, but we need to know who and what we're dealing with here. Start at the beginning."

So, I do, and it's painfully embarrassing. "I saw him last week at the store, and he followed me around and grabbed my arm. I ran out of there and straight into Nevin."

"And Nevin didn't handle him?"

"Nevin didn't know until Chad was already long gone."

Thomas scrubs his hand across his face. "We'll handle him."

"What are you going to do?" I ask.

"I can almost guarantee you aren't the first woman he's done something to, and I'm going to find out and do whatever we need to so you're the last."

I stare at my Uncle Thomas and then look at Uncle James, waiting for one of them to say something else.

When they don't, I ask. "And that is?"

Uncle James shakes his head. "Don't worry about it. He won't be an issue anymore."

"You don't know that," I fire back.

"I can promise you that," Uncle James replies, tapping his index finger on his desk.

Uncle Thomas stands and touches my shoulder, smiling down at me as I peer up. "But to be safe, either go stay with your parents for a few days or have someone stay with you."

"I'll stay with you," Trace offers, but he's about as helpful as a broomstick to keep me safe.

"I'll call Nevin and ask him to stay with me a few days," I tell him, but I fucking hate this shit.

"Good. Just a few days," he says to me. "You'll never see Chad again."

I gape at them and am filled with so many questions. None of which they'll answer.

I have a feeling Chad isn't long for this world, and I don't feel bad about it either. He is a predator and is about to become the prey.

21

NEVIN

"ARE YOU GOING TO TALK TO ME OR PRETEND I'M NOT here?"

Luna stares at the television from the other end of the couch. "I'm talking."

"Sure," I whisper. "We need to talk about what happened."

"My uncles are taking care of him."

I turn my entire body toward her. "You know I'm not talking about that."

She stares back at me, looking clueless and innocent. "I don't know what you're talking about."

"I hurt your feelings."

I didn't mean to, but I know when I said we were only friends after sleeping with her that my words stung.

Her face doesn't change. "When?"

"At your grandparents'."

She blinks a few times and continues to stare at me.

"I don't remember anything," she says before turning her gaze back toward the television.

I slide across the couch until our hips touch. She doesn't move away from me, but she doesn't lean in either.

"Luna, look at me," I plead with her, but she doesn't even give me the side-eye. "What are we to each other?"

She shrugs but doesn't open her mouth to answer the question.

"Are we friends?"

"Sure," she whispers.

"Are we lovers?"

"We were."

Those words are like a punch to the gut.

We were.

"I'm shit at this," I admit.

"Yep. You are."

I reach over and place my hand on top of hers. "I'm sorry, Luna."

"It's fine," she mumbles.

I may be naïve and dumb when it comes to women, but I know the word fine means things are anything but fine.

"I don't know how to act around you. I'm totally clueless. I said one stupid thing, and now you're giving me the cold shoulder."

She nods. "I'll get over it."

"When?"

"It'll be a while."

I groan. "What should I have said when asked? Should I have said you were mine? Is that what you wanted me to say in front of your entire family before we even had a chance to talk about what either of us wanted?"

She doesn't answer.

"Is that what you wanted? Should I have told them we fucked a few times and now you are my bitch?"

I know I've crossed the line. I know my words are going to piss her off. But I want her to be mad. I want her to act. Anything is better than the indifferent silent treatment she is giving me.

But the one thing I don't expect is for her to lunge at me, raising her hand like she is going to strike me.

"Shut the fuck up!" she yells in my face as I grab her arms, stopping her from hitting me. "You're a fucking asshole." She struggles to free herself, yanking and pushing against my grip.

"Never said I wasn't, Lu." I pull her arms down, pinning them behind her back with one hand.

She slides forward, wrestling with me and managing to shove her breasts in my face. Using my free hand, I wrap it around her waist and haul her into my lap.

"Calm down," I tell her, wanting to de-escalate the situation and not knowing that's not what you want to say to a woman when you want them to hear you out and talk.

"Fuck you!" she screams in my face. "And fuck everyone."

I don't know what to do except one thing. I lean forward, crushing my mouth against hers. She jostles in my lap and only struggles for a moment before she kisses me back.

Her lips are punishing in their pursuit of mine. She is filled with rage and is taking it out on me, kissing me back with so much ferocity, I can barely breathe.

I grip her hands tighter, holding her captive as our tongues move in sync. I get lost in her, drowning in her taste, her smell, and the feel of her body pressed against mine.

The woman is so infuriating and intriguing at the same time, I can't stop myself from wanting more. She's unlike anyone I've ever met before and nothing like the little girl I barely knew when I was young.

"Nevin," she breathes against my lips.

I release her hands, wanting them roaming my body and needing her touch. I moan as she slides her hands across my neck, resting her fingers on my back.

She pulls back, and I think it's over. The moment has passed. Fuck. I shouldn't have let her hands go.

"I'm sorry," she says, staring me in the eye. "I'm so, so sorry."

"I'm sorry, Luna."

She leans forward, placing her forehead against mine. "I think I'm falling for you," she admits, closing her eyes. "And that scares me to death."

"Me too," I confess. "I've never felt this way about anyone before you, but don't be scared."

She places her palm flat on my chest and leans into me. "My uncles are out there doing God knows what, and what if something happens to them or to you?"

"Why would something happen to me?" I glide my arm around her waist, holding her again. "I'm not going anywhere."

"I don't know. Anything can happen."

"Babe," I whisper and kiss her forehead. "Going to take something really big to tear me away from you. We just found each other, and I'm not giving that up without a fight."

"But what if Chad…"

I move my hand from her cheek to her lips. "He's a nonissue."

"He is an issue," she mumbles against my fingers. "Especially now that everyone's involved and he found my uncle. That wasn't by chance."

"He won't get near you. I'm not scared of Chad."

"He's a maniac. If he tries to do something to you…" She squeezes her eyes shut. "I don't know what I'd do."

"He'll be handled."

"Don't go and try to be heroic again."

I pull her closer, cupping her jaw in my hand. "I'll always protect the people I care the most about, and that includes you now, Lu. I'll give everything I've got to keep you safe, and not because Ian asked me to, but because I want to… I need to."

She relaxes in my embrace. "But if you ever call me a bitch again…"

"Whoa. Whoa." I shake my head and hold in a laugh. "I didn't call you a bitch."

"I'm not *your* bitch either."

"Got it. Loud and clear, li'l moon."

"We're dating."

"Exclusively?" I ask.

"Uh, yeah." She nibbles on the corner of her lip. "I've never been in a relationship, though. We're going to fuck this up big-time."

I don't hold it in anymore and laugh softly. "Lu, I've never been in one either."

"No? I thought maybe you had a long-term relationship with someone in prison."

"Babe," I mutter through my laughter. "I've never been anyone's bitch either. I also don't have a fucking clue what I'm doing."

"We'll go slow and be gentle with each other."

"Please. I like going slow with you," I say with a smirk.

"Then kiss me slow and fuck me slower," she demands, and my cock comes to life, wanting exactly what she said.

I stand, taking her with me as she wraps her legs around my waist. I plan to spend all night giving her so much pleasure she has no time to think of anything else.

We're two paces down the hallway when there's a

pounding at the door. Luna freezes and pulls her lips away.

"Luna, open the door," her father barks and continues his pounding.

"Fuck," she whispers with wide eyes as her legs squeeze my body so tight, I can barely breathe. "I'm in so much trouble." She slides down my body and slowly turns toward the door, wiping her lips as she walks.

I move to the couch, taking the seat I'd sat in before our blowout. But I have wood. Not a little bit of wood, but a massive boner. I grab a pillow from the other end, placing it over my lap.

"Daddy," Luna says cheerfully as she opens the door. "What's wrong?"

"What's wrong?" he asks, stalking into the apartment with his shoulders squared and his jaw set. "What's wrong?"

"Yeah. What's wrong?" She glances at me, playing everything off. "We were just watching a movie."

He peers down at her and takes a deep breath, trying to hold his shit together. I know the look well. I've worn it a time or two. "Who's Chad?"

"Don't be mad," she begs him.

"Baby girl, I'm not mad at you. I'm worried. There's a difference. You're my daughter, and I'm hurt you didn't tell me someone was bothering you."

She steps forward and wraps her arms around her father's waist. "I can't tell you about every weirdo."

"Yeah, you can. It's my job to protect you."

She peers up at him. "Dad, I'm grown."

"I don't care how old you are. You'll always be my little girl, Luna."

"Crazy," she whispers, hugging him tightly.

He touches her shoulders and pushes her back a little. "Tell me about Chad, honey."

"Want to sit down?" she asks him.

It's then that he sees me. I ready myself for a new round of anger, but he gives me a chin lift followed by a "Hey," which totally fucks with my head.

He follows her to the sitting area and takes the empty chair next to the couch. As soon as she sits down, he grabs her hand and speaks softly. "What happened?"

"He's a guy I went on one date with, but he's been popping up and hasn't stopped calling and texting me. He doesn't understand the word no."

"Why didn't you tell me about him?"

She shrugs. "I figured he'd go away."

"You were going to run when you saw him at ALFA too, weren't you?"

She nods.

Fuck me. Even when confronted with the asshole at her uncle's office, she still wasn't going to spill the tea on Chad and his dickhead behavior. Luna and I are going to have a talk about personal safety and when to believe someone is a threat.

"Always tell someone."

"I don't want anyone to get hurt," she tells him, to which he groans.

Same, buddy. Same.

"She didn't tell me either," I say, wanting him to know.

That statement earns me a handful of eye daggers thrown my way. "Shut it," she chirps.

"Promise me, you'll tell someone…anyone, from now on."

"I promise, Dad."

Mr. Gallo peers over at me. "Chad's in the wind. MIA. Luna's going to come home with me until we find him."

"No," she barks, not letting him finish the statement or me to answer. "I'm not going home with you. This is my home, and I'm staying here."

"You'll be safer there than you are alone."

Luna raises her chin. "I'm not alone."

Mr. Gallo looks at me again, studying me, and then stares at her. "Fuck," he groans. "You two a thing now?"

I'm not saying shit. I got myself into trouble with Luna last time someone asked that same question, and I am not about to dig a hole with her father by being honest.

"We're dating, Dad. I feel safe with him. If anyone's going to protect me, it'll be him."

"I believe he will, Luna," he says while looking directly at me. He scrubs his hand down his face and groans. "After we almost lost your sister, though, I think it's best if—"

"No," Luna tells him point-blank.

"I won't leave her side," I promise. "Not for a second until Chad's behind bars and no longer a risk. I'd lay down my life for her, Mr. Gallo."

Mr. Gallo cocks his head and doesn't take his eyes off me. "Not for a second?"

"Not for a second," I repeat.

He tips his head back, cursing under his breath for a few seconds before he looks at his daughter again. "Why are you three girls so impossible and hardheaded?"

Luna smiles at him. "You made us this way, Dad."

He grumbles some more before turning his attention toward me. "Keep her safe, or you better run. My kids and my wife are the most important things in my life."

"I promise, sir."

No one ever talked about my brothers and me that way. I wonder what we'd be like if someone had? I wouldn't be the same man I am now. Maybe I'd be a shit human, but hearing those words at least once would be something else.

Luna turns toward me. "I'm going to walk him out," she says.

"I'll wait at the door," I tell her, knowing her dad won't want her alone even for a minute.

"Don't be ridic..." she starts to say until her father puts his hand on her shoulder.

"Good," he says to me, ignoring her. "Don't let her out of your sight."

"I hate this," Luna mutters.

Her dad smiles down at her, not caring if she likes it or not. "I want you alive. Now, walk me out."

She walks out the door first, and he gives me a look, one I can feel in my bones. Luna has tried him his entire life, and this is just another moment when he's showing exactly how much patience he has. I don't know if I'd be the same in his shoes, but he somehow pulls it off as calmly as possible.

I give him a chin lift, and he returns the gesture before following Luna out the front door. I trail behind, never leaving the entryway as they talk and walk to the parking lot.

Without being told, I know the next few days are going to be a struggle. Luna will make sure of it.

22

LUNA

I'M CRABBY. NOT JUST A LITTLE, BUT A WHOLE LOT. It's been three days since Chad disappeared, and Nevin hasn't let me out of his sight. He's taking the role and responsibility very seriously, and it's annoying. No one has watched over me so much since my father did before I moved out of my parents' house.

"You may as well get your things from the Wayward," I tell Nevin, lying sideways on my recliner, letting my legs dangle over the arm. "Doesn't seem like you're going anywhere anytime soon."

Nevin turns around with the container of milk in one hand and the butter in the other and stares at me. "I still don't think it's a good idea, Luna."

I sigh, feeling a bit dramatic and bored. "No reason to pay for a place you're never at, and at the rate we're going, you're never going to be there again."

Nevin shakes his head, returning to cooking. "A little over the top, aren't ya?"

"Not one bit." I watch as his back and shoulder muscles move as he stirs the boiling noodles. "And to be honest, it hasn't been a hardship having you around either."

He's taken up cooking. Something the food at my grandmother's must've sparked. I can't say I hate it because I'm getting a break from my normal processed-food rotation.

"You think you can put too much cheese in mac and cheese?" he asks me.

"No such thing as too much cheese, Nev."

He reaches to his side, opening the fridge without having to move the few steps. I wish I were that big; it would make life so much easier. "Cheesy mac is what we're going to call this, because I'm going to drown the bitch."

"Did you find the recipe online?" I ask him, wondering where he's finding the inspiration.

"I got it from your grandmother when we were there last time."

I sit up a little straighter, wondering how I missed that interaction. "You what?"

He nods without turning around. "I ate an entire plate of it after the hurricane, and she gave me the recipe."

"And you're just whipping it up, thinking you can cook something so complicated?"

He spins around, staring at me like I'm not normal. "There are directions, Lu. It involves boiling and stirring."

I shrug, knowing what it involves, but also knowing the dishes always end up like garbage when I'm the cook. "You think it's easy, but it's not."

My phone rings before Nevin has a chance to reply. "Hello," I say without looking at who's on the other end.

"Lu."

My heart jumps at the sound of the familiar voice. "Ian? Oh my God, is that you. Are you okay?" I say, rushing all the words out without giving him a chance to reply to anything. "I've been so worried."

Nevin drops everything on the counter and rushes to my side. "Ian," he says, not thinking.

"Nevin?" Ian says, and it's hard to miss the surprise in his voice.

"Where are you guys?" Ian asks us.

"We're at Luna's," Nevin tells him.

"Oh," Ian replies.

"It's a long story, but the short version is someone is bothering me and Nevin's been tasked with babysitting," I explain.

"It's not like that," Nevin argues, giving me the stink eye.

"It's exactly like that," I say, narrowing my eyes at him.

"Who's after you? What the hell is happening over

there?" Ian asks, and I hate that my best friend isn't around to tell everything to.

"Some random dude I went on a date with. His name is Chad."

Ian growls. "I remember you talking about him after the date. He's coming around?"

"He's missing right now," I say.

Nevin takes the phone from my hand, and I lurch forward, trying to get it back, but I fail. I stare at Nevin as he marches back into the kitchen with my phone, setting it next to the stove as he checks on the noodles. "The guy showed up at ALFA. Luna freaked and tipped off her uncles. They're searching for him, but someone had to make sure she was protected, and I'm staying here until we know she's safe."

"Don't leave her alone for a minute," Ian tells him, much to my surprise. "She doesn't always think about her safety, and I don't want to be here and worried about her at the same time."

"I got you, brother," Nevin says to Ian.

"You two getting along okay?" Ian asks.

"We're good. She's good. I'm good. We're good," Nevin repeats. "How are you?"

Ian doesn't answer right away. "You two a thing now?" he asks Nevin.

This time, Nevin is the one who doesn't answer right away, and he stops stirring his dumb noodles. "I don't…"

"It's okay if you are. You both deserve good people,

and there's no one else I'd trust with my best friend more than you, brother. It's just that…"

"That what?" Nevin asks.

"I wish I were there with you."

"I ain't into that shit," Nevin tells Ian.

Ian laughs. "Dumbass, I didn't mean it that way. I just feel like everyone's living while I'm…"

"I get it. I get it better than anyone."

I sit there in shock. I was worried about Ian finding out about what is happening between Nevin and me, and he doesn't even seem the least bit fazed by any of it.

"Anyone bothering you?" Nevin asks.

"Not yet. I'm barely settled in. Trying to figure out who to trust and who not to."

"Trust no one. Not even the guards," Nevin tells him. "I mean that too, Ian. No one."

"No one," Ian repeats.

"No one is your friend."

"I feel it."

"Just keep your nose clean so you can get home to us sooner," Nevin says, reaching for the oven mitts.

"That's my plan."

When Nevin has the boiling pot of water in his hands, I use the opportunity to take the phone back. "He's emptying the boiling water," I tell Ian.

"Boiling water?"

I stalk toward my bedroom, leaving Nevin to finish his concoction. "He's making mac and cheese. He thinks he's Emeril or something."

"Anything he makes will be a hell of a lot better than the slop in here," Ian says, sounding so far away.

I collapse onto my bed, staring up at the ceiling. "Are you really okay with this?"

"With what?"

God, he's dense and impossible at the same time.

"With Nevin being here?"

"Luna, you're grown. He's grown too. You're my best friend, and all I want is good things for you. Why would I be upset?"

I exhale and close my eyes. "I don't know. I just thought…"

"Are you happy?"

"Kind of."

"Kind of?" he asks.

"You're not here. I'm pretty miserable without my friend."

"Best friend," Ian corrects me. "As long as you don't give Nevin that title, I'm good."

I smile, but then remember he's not at his place; he's in prison. It's not like I forgot, but it is still so foreign and unbelievable. "Are you really okay? Is it awful?"

"It's definitely not a vacation, but…" He pauses, covering the phone to talk to someone else. "Sorry. It's given me a lot of time to think."

"And?"

"I hate that my brother lived this way for something I did."

"I know," I whisper. "But the only person who

deserves to be behind bars is dead. You don't deserve it either."

"I'll survive," he says, and I know if anyone can, it's Ian. "My cellmate isn't a total douchebag."

"What's he in for?"

"Drugs."

"Better than murder."

"Ain't that the truth," he mumbles.

"I feel guilty, Ian."

"For what?"

"For liking Nevin."

"Babe, if I could pick anyone in the world for you to be with, it would be my brother. It means you'll always be in my life, and I know you're with a good person who can and will take care of you."

"I can take care of myself," I argue.

There's silence.

"Well, I can," I insist.

"Sure."

He covers the phone again, talking to someone else before giving his attention back to me. "I've got to go. I'll call again soon, and you should get a letter in the mail from me any day now. It has my address. Write to me."

"I will," I promise.

"I love you, Luna. Tell Nevin I love him too."

I fight back the tears that are threatening to fall. "I love you too, Ian. Stay safe."

"I will. Later, Lu."

"Later, Ian," I whisper, unable to speak any louder.

Ian hangs up, and I sit there for a good thirty seconds, wiping away the tears from my eyes. It has to be harder for him than me. I have other people and things around me to pass the time and fill my days, while Ian has nothing and no one.

"Luna," Nevin calls out from the kitchen. "Ian still on the phone?"

"No," I call back, pushing myself to stand and head out of the bedroom.

I'm not even a few feet out of my bedroom when the smell hits me. My mouth instantly waters as my stomach grumbles. There's absolutely no way it'll taste as good as it smells. It's impossible for melted cheese to give off any other aroma than sheer bliss, but I'm still doubtful of how it'll all pull together.

Nevin's standing at the island with two bowls filled to the top and steam coming off. "It's ready."

"Did you taste it?" I ask, climbing up on a stool across from him.

"No. I'm saving the honor for you." He smiles, looking so damn proud. "Is Ian okay?"

"I think so. He sounded like Ian."

"Is he pissed about us?"

I shake my head as I lift the spoon. "Not that I can tell."

"Well, you'd know if he was better than me."

I know Ian better than any of his brothers do, and he's a straight shooter. He's never held back with me.

We've always been honest with each other, even if it's brutal.

"I think he's fine." I don't know if I'm trying to convince myself out of guilt or if he truly sounded okay with Nevin and me hanging out and being together on a physical level. "He's fine."

"Did he say he wasn't?"

I shake my head, moving the macaroni and cheese around in my bowl.

"Men rarely say the opposite of what they mean, Lu. If he said it's cool, then it's cool."

I glance up from the bowl. "Why do I feel bad?"

Nevin leans over, letting the steam waft up into his face. "Don't know. Maybe because he isn't here. If you want to walk things back a little, I'll understand."

"No," I say quickly. "I don't. Ian and I weren't that way."

"Then stop acting like you're cheating on my brother with me. It's freaking me out. Eat." He dips his chin and gaze to my bowl. "Tell me if it's shit."

"I'm going to be the guinea pig?"

He nods.

"Fuck," I mutter, stabbing at the noodles, bracing myself for complete disappointment.

Nevin keeps his gaze trained on me as I lift a forkful to my lips, blowing on the food so the melted cheese doesn't burn my mouth.

"Here goes nothing," I say, hoping I don't have to lie about the taste.

Nevin looks so hopeful as I place the fork in my mouth, slowly closing my lips. I chew and stop and chew again. Damn. The different tastes of cheddar, butter, and other things I can't pinpoint explode against my tongue. It's creamy perfection, and I hate Nevin for how easily he pulled it off.

"Well?" He studies my face, trying to read me.

"It's good," I mumble with my mouth still full.

His shoulders fall. "Just good?"

I swallow and lick my lips. "It's amazing, actually. I ain't going to lie, I wanted it to be meh."

His eyebrows rise. "You wanted it to be meh?"

I nod. "Only because I couldn't do it and somehow you could."

"Babe, I eat. You eat. It's a win-win no matter who made it."

"It's impressive for your first time. My grandma would be proud."

He perks up. "You think she would be?"

I nod. "Eat it. You'll see. It's just as good as hers."

"Impossible," he mutters before placing a forkful in his mouth too. He chews, and I can see when it hits him…he did good.

"See?"

He smiles. "It's good, but not as good as your grandma's."

"This is nice," I say to him, my crabbiness and guilt melting away.

"What?"

"This." I wave my hand between us. "Us."

He smiles, making my belly flip a little. "Best few weeks I've had in my entire life, Lu."

I'm both honored and horrified by that statement. The weeks have been good, but also totally mundane besides the hurricane.

"I'm sorry," I whisper, pushing the mac and cheese around again.

"Babe," he says. "Look at me."

I peer up, my blue eyes meeting his green.

"Don't be sorry. I'm happy. My past is my past, but I'm most excited about the future, and I couldn't say that too long ago. It's because of you."

I try to push away the sadness, knowing Nevin has so much in front of himself, whether it includes me or not. "It'll only get better."

He shakes his head. "If this is all there is, I'll be content for the rest of my life."

"It has been nice," I confirm. "Even if there's a lunatic out there looking for me."

"I'm pretty sure he's trying to save his ass. He knows he fucked up. As soon as he shows his face, he'll no longer be an issue for you."

I set my fork down, suddenly no longer happy. "You think they'll find him?"

"Yeah. He can't hide for long."

"Yeah," I whisper. My uncles are a force. If anyone can find him, they can.

"You going to work tonight?" Nevin asks, chowing

down on his mac and cheese.

"I am. I can't miss tonight. I have a client coming in who's been booked for months."

"I'll take you and stay."

I shake my head. "I won't be alone. You have to work. I'll be fine."

He stares at me, chewing. "I don't know."

"Nevin, don't be ridiculous. Everyone will be there. If I'm not safe with my family, who am I safe with?"

He continues chewing, tilting his head. "I'll drop you off and pick you up."

I don't bother arguing. There's no point. My dad put him in charge of my protection, and Nevin's taking the responsibility a little too seriously. "Fine."

"I don't like it, though. I want that known."

"Noted, big guy." I slide off the stool, taking the bowl with me. "I'm going to get ready. We'll leave in an hour."

"I'm ready when you are," he says.

I turn around as I make it to the hallway. "Thank you for this." I hold up the bowl. "It's great."

"Just trying to help you grow those perfect tits, babe."

I laugh, loving that he remembered my stupid statement. "We'll have to see if it's working."

"I plan on it." He winks.

23

NEVIN

I park Dylan's bike in front of Inked and walk inside, looking for Luna. "Where is she?" I ask.

"Well, hello to you too," Arlo says as she sits at the front desk, rubbing her belly.

"Hey," I clip out, trying to be cordial to her family in a moment when I could give a shit about niceties. "Luna?"

Arlo ticks her head toward the back. "She finished up a few minutes ago. I'm guessing she's in the back room."

I curl my fingers into a fist as I fight the nagging feeling that followed me the entire way over here from the bar. "You're guessing?"

"I can't keep tabs on all of them," Arlo says as I stalk by her toward the back of the shop.

"Hey," Ro says as soon as she lifts her head and her gaze lands on me. "Here for your pickup?"

I glance around, not seeing Luna anywhere. "She back there?" I tip my head toward the storage room.

"She went back there a few minutes ago to stock up for tomorrow," Ro says, going back to tattooing her client.

I keep moving, not bothering with more small talk. I had my fill of people at the bar and want to grab Luna and head home.

I stop, realizing what just went through my mind. *Home.* Luna feels like home. Not her apartment or the other people around me, although I like them. Luna herself has quickly become home to me.

I push open the door to the stock room, but it's empty. My heart sinks, and panic immediately sets in. "Luna!" I yell out, moving back to the middle of the shop.

Ro's up on her feet, tattoo gun in her hand. "She's not back there?"

"No."

Ro's face turns white. "Fuck," she hisses, dropping the gun on her side table.

I don't wait. Don't have anything else to say. Luna wasn't out front, and the only other place she could be is out back. I run toward the back, punching open the door.

The back parking lot is dark with only a few cars. Luna's truck is under the streetlight off to the right, and I can hear noises coming from that general direction. I haul ass with Rosie on my heels—and no doubt the rest of Luna's family close behind her.

My stomach twists as I brace myself for what I'm about to find. Every horrible scenario runs through my head. I imagine Luna on the ground, bleeding and broken at the hands of Chad. If he touches one hair on her head...

When I make it to the other side of the truck, I stop dead in my tracks. Luna's covered in blood, standing over a man who has his face buried in the gravel.

Our eyes connect, and I see relief flood her features as she doubles over. She gasps for air, hands on her knees, and sways back and forth.

I rush to her side, holding her up. "Are you okay?"

"I'm okay," she whispers as her body shakes in my arms.

"Oh, dear God," Ro says from off to the side. "What the..."

I push Luna's back against the truck, careful not to hurt her. I lift her shirt over her stomach and then move on to her arms.

"What are you doing?" she asks softly.

"Looking for where all the blood is coming from," I tell her, my voice so panicked, it may be shaking more than she is.

"It's his," she tells me.

I pull back, staring up at her face, which has some blood splatter on it too. "It's his?" There's no hiding the shock in my voice.

She nods. "It's Chad's."

I glance over my shoulder as Carmello kneels down,

rolling Chad onto his back. A loud groan falls from Chad's lips, and Carmello gasps.

"Holy fuck," Carmello says. "That's brutal."

"Don't let him move," I tell Luna's cousin.

Carmello looks up at me, shaking his head. "The man isn't going anywhere except a hospital, Nev. He's fucked up, and not just fucked up, fucked up—but fucked up, fucked up."

"Good," I say, turning my full attention back to Luna.

She places her hands on my shoulders, steadying herself. "He deserved it."

I brush the hair away from her face. "He did, baby. He did."

She stumbles forward, wrapping her arms around my body, and I catch her, clutching her to my front. "Someone call Joe."

"On it," Ro says, already with her phone to her ear. "Dad. Come to Inked. Chad's here." Then she pauses. "Just get here as soon as possible."

"I'll call my dad too," Carmello says, pulling out his phone but staying at Chad's side.

"Is he going to die?" Luna whispers as she looks up at me.

"No, sweetheart. He's not going to die," I reassure her. "His ego is probably the most damaged thing on him."

She smiles, nuzzling against my chest. "Doubtful.

I'm pretty sure he's never going to father children with the way I kicked him with these spiked heels right in his nuts. They're probably lodged somewhere around his colon right now."

I wince, hating the imagery but loving that she beat his ass. "You're crazy fearless, Luna. You could've been hurt."

"Or I could be dead," she whispers, closing her eyes. "But he's the one on the ground and not me. I'll take crazy fearless any day of the week."

I tip my head forward, brushing a kiss on her forehead. "Me too, li'l moon." I pull down the tailgate of her truck and climb up while keeping her tight in my arms. "Your dad is coming."

"Good," she says, her eyes still closed, but shaking less than she was a minute ago.

"Are you sure you aren't hurt?" I ask her, looking all over her body but not even seeing a scratch on her.

"He grabbed me by the arm when I ran out here to get something from my truck. I didn't even look to see who it was before I elbowed him, and he dropped. From there…it gets a little fuzzy until the nut kick."

I growl. "You came out here alone?"

"Yeah."

"Why would you do that?" I try to not sound like I'm chastising her, but I sure as fuck am.

"I needed something."

"Luna," I clip out. "Maybe I was wrong about the

crazy fearlessness. What in God's name were you thinking?"

She pushes herself up in my arms. "I didn't think he'd be out here."

"Fuck," I groan. "Your dad is going to kill me."

"Kill you?" she says, laughing. "He's going to kill me."

"Baby, it was my job to—"

She places her bloodied finger against my lips. "I'm a grown-ass woman, Nevin. I'm in charge of me and no one else."

I growl again, unable to hide my agitation, but it's not anger. If something would've happened to her... I can't even allow myself to think it. "Don't do that shit anymore, Lu. I know you're grown and you can take care of yourself, but fuck...if one thing would've happened differently—"

"But it didn't."

A motorcycle pulls into the back lot, sending cinders everywhere. Her father's eyes are moving around the scene as he climbs off the bike, but before his leg swings over the seat, Mrs. Gallo is running in our direction. Joe zeroes in on Luna as she sits in my arms.

"She's okay," I call out, reassuring them.

"Oh my God. My baby," Mrs. G says, rushing to Luna's truck. Her hand moves to Luna's face, cupping her cheek. "Are you hurt?"

Luna shakes her head, turning toward her mother.

"I'm okay, Mom. This isn't mine." She's talking about the blood. And for it not being hers, there's plenty of it.

"Sweet Jesus," her mother mutters, checking over her daughter. "You could've died."

"But I didn't," Luna tells her.

Mrs. Gallo sucks in a breath, looking like she's holding on by a thread. "So reckless, baby. So reckless."

"I'm not reckless, Mom. I walked to my truck, but at least I knew what to do."

"He's here," Carmello tells Joe, pointing down at the man who's rolling around in pain. "She beat him pretty badly."

"Fuckin' good," Luna's father says. "He deserves it." Joe stands over the man, taking in his injuries. He's unfazed by the amount of blood, which is both troubling and worrisome.

"Want me to call the cops?" Ro asks her father.

Joe shakes his head. "Wait for James. He'll handle them."

"I have the best family," Luna says to me, curling back against my front.

I stare at them all working together, soaking in their concern for everyone involved. She does have the best family. She was lucky the day she was born. She never experienced abuse like I did. She doesn't even know what it feels like to be alone. She'll never have to with the number of people who fill her world.

"You do, baby. You do."

Mrs. G pulls Luna's top half into an embrace while she's still on my lap. It's only mildly awkward, but sweet too. "Thank goodness you knew how to protect yourself, baby."

Her mother's eyes meet mine, but I look away, feeling as if I've somehow failed. "I'm sorry, Mrs. Gallo," I say softly.

"Hey," she says, releasing Luna.

I don't look at her. I can't. I should've kept her daughter safe enough that she wouldn't have had to defend herself.

"Hey," she says again, but this time I look at her. As soon as our gazes lock, she keeps talking. "You did your best. Luna never listens. It's always been her thing. If there's trouble, she's going to find it, or it's going to find her. You did nothing wrong, Nevin."

"Okay," I whisper, but the knot in my stomach doesn't unfurl.

"I mean. You did nothing. Don't blame yourself for this." She waves her hand toward the man on the ground. "You'll learn about my sweet girl the longer you're with her. This wasn't your fault," she says again. "If you blame yourself for all the trouble that finds her, you're going to feel guilty your entire life."

"Mom, come on now," Luna says, shaking her head. "I'm not that bad."

Her mother's eyes swing her way, and she raises an eyebrow. "If my hair weren't so blond, you'd see all the gray hair you and your sisters have given me."

Luna rolls her eyes. "That's not from us. That's Dad's fault."

"Oh, he has an entire section too," Mrs. Gallo says with a small laugh. "Y'all are trying my sanity at times."

Joe stalks our way, his eyes on his daughter. I don't know what to do. Do I put her down? Do I hold her tighter?

"Baby," he says softly, placing his arm around his wife's back and his hand on her hip. "You okay? Look at me."

She turns in my arms to face her father. "Hey, Daddy," she says, sounding so small and fragile. Two things I've learned she isn't.

"You okay?" he asks her again as his gaze roams her face and her body for visible injuries.

"He didn't touch me. This is all his blood."

Joe's eyebrows rise, thinking the same thing I did. Impressive. "All of it is his?"

She nods. "I did everything you taught me."

"Never knew you really listened, baby girl."

"She's like her father," Mrs. Gallo says, shaking her head.

Luna smiles again. "I did."

"How did he get you?" he asks her.

I brace myself. I know if I was pissed at her stupid move, he is about to lose his goddamn mind.

"I came out here to get—"

He tips his head, furrowing his brows. "Want to say that again? I think I heard you wrong."

"Nope," I bite out. "You didn't."

She winces. "I needed something from my truck."

He runs his hand across his jaw, smashing his teeth together. "Fuck me. You could've been killed. For what? Some damn lip gloss?"

She rolls her eyes, sitting up a little straighter in my lap. "No. I don't wear lip gloss. I wanted to change my shoes. My feet were killing me in these damn heels that men designed as torture devices."

He kicks at the cinders, holding back his anger. "And you didn't think to have anyone escort you out here in the dark?"

"I shouldn't need an escort, but Chad had to be the tool he is, or at least was, and what did he get? His ass whooped by a girl," she says, her voice getting louder with each subsequent word. "I refuse to be held captive because a man who's clearly delusional can't take no for an answer."

Joe grunts, cursing under his breath. "I'm sorry, Luna. I'm not mad at you, baby. I'm pissed you even had to deal with this shit and then you had to take matters into your own hands."

He says those last words while looking at me.

"I found her out here."

"You were a few minutes too late," he snaps.

I want to be pissed at his attitude, but I get it. I really

do. He's upset and lashing out at the only person who can take it.

"Dad, you know it's my fault. Don't be mad at Nevin," Luna says, coming to my defense.

He blows out a breath before his face softens. "I'm not mad at anyone, Luna. I'm scared. It's different. It's going to take me more than a few minutes to calm my ass down. I drove over here thinking you were hurt or worse."

"I'm sorry," she whispers.

"Don't be sorry." He reaches out, taking her chin between his fingers. "I'm proud of you."

Her chin stops trembling. I don't know if it's from his touch or his words. "Thanks, Daddy."

I'd be lying if I didn't admit I was jealous of their relationship. Really, any of her family relationships. I realize how empty my life has been since the day I was born.

"And you," he says, turning his gaze on me. "You did good, son. You did the best you could with a wild one like her. She never makes anything easy."

"I'm sorry, sir," I tell him again.

He gives me a chin lift. "Don't be. I know you did your best, and that's all I can ask."

It sounds nice, but I know if something had happened to her tonight, I'd be the one paying for it. If not through the courts, then at the hands of her father and uncles.

A dark Challenger pulls into the parking lot, sending

cinders everywhere, just like Joe's bike did. It's as if they all took a course in how to make a grand and dramatic entrance.

"Oh boy," Mrs. Gallo mutters, turning to see Luna's uncle unfold his big body from such a low car.

James is out of his car, moving toward Chad's body. "He alive?"

Carmello greets his father before he makes it all the way to Chad. "He's alive. Stable, but fucked up."

"Fucked up is perfect." James's eyes turn toward us. "She okay?"

"She's fine," Joe answers for her.

James has his phone out and is tapping on the screen. "My buddy from the Marshals is on the way."

"Marshals?" Carmello asks, looking back at Chad.

"The perp is wanted on drug charges and a rape in another state five years ago."

"Shit," I groan, suddenly imagining how very badly this could've gone.

"Pretty sure he won't be using his dick for a long time," Luna says, sounding more confident than she did a few minutes ago. "I made sure of that."

"Good girl," James says, smiling at his niece. "Those shoes have their upside."

She wiggles her feet. "They're weapons, for sure."

"We're going to retire those," I whisper in her ear.

She peers up at me. "No way in hell. I hate how they feel, but they have their purpose and served me well tonight."

"Maybe we should put them in a shadow box on a shelf in your apartment like a memento of the first ass you kicked."

She laughs. "Baby," she calls out to me, melting my insides. "He wasn't the first, and neither was Oliver."

Fuck. I forgot about Oliver. "He wasn't your first either?"

She shakes her head. "But I'm hoping Chad will be my last."

"Me fucking too."

"Keep an eye on her," Joe says as he stalks toward James, all parties standing over Chad, but no one helping him.

Ro and Gigi head toward us, coming to check on their sister.

"You need anything? Water?" Ro asks Luna.

Luna looks down at her hands. "A towel would be nice."

Ro's heading toward the shop without a second thought or asking more questions.

Gigi winces when her eyes finally take in the sight of her sister. "Where did all the blood come from?"

"I may have sat on his chest and punched him a couple of times in the face, and his nose took a shot or two. It leaked like a sieve."

Gigi clutches her stomach, turning green. "You're too much."

"You know what it's like when someone attacks

you. You go into a totally different mode," Luna says to her elder sister.

Gigi nods. "I wasn't all Rambo like you, though."

There's so much to these sisters. More than I ever imagined. They aren't shy little things, and they know how to protect themselves, which is something we were never taught but had to figure out on our own.

"I think you all need to hang up your boxing gloves," I say to them.

They both turn their gazes on me. Luna's the first to speak. "If men didn't start shit with us, we wouldn't have to bring out the big guns," she says, having a sense of humor even though she was just attacked.

Thankfully, he only grabbed her arm, and her instinct was to fight back. He didn't have time to hurt her before she put his ass on the ground. If she hadn't reacted so fast, we would be dealing with something far different, and no one would be joking about anything.

A police car pulls into the parking lot, moving at a normal speed and not sending gravel everywhere like the older Gallo men.

"Here we go," Luna whispers. "You think this will take long?"

I shake my head. "Probably just a statement."

"I want you to take me home," Luna says to me, relaxing in my lap. "I'm tired."

"The adrenaline is wearing off," I say to her, holding her tighter so I can become her support. "We'll get you tucked in."

Ro's back with a towel in her hand and a spray bottle. "I grabbed some alcohol too so you can sanitize your hands," she says as she hands the white towel to her sister.

Luna holds her hands out for Ro to spray. "Thanks, sissy."

"You're welcome, Lu. You scared me for a hot minute," Ro says.

"I'm not going out that easy," Luna replies.

I let them have their moment, concentrating on the police as they speak with Luna's father and uncle. They keep their gaze pinned on Chad, who not only hasn't found his footing yet, but is also being held down by Carmello to make sure he stays where he is.

It's funny. When I walked out of prison, I thought life would be calm. I thought I'd struggle to fit in somewhere and have nothing to my name, but it wouldn't matter because at least I'd have peace and solitude.

None of that's been true, and I'm more than okay with it. I have more people in my life than I ever imagined possible. People who seem to like and care for me, although I've done nothing to earn it.

Do I think any of them would take a bullet for me? I haven't gotten to that point yet, but I know if I got into a jam, I could probably call on anyone in Luna's family and they'd have my back in a heartbeat.

When I was young and hated the Gallos, specifically Joe, because he was an asshole, I never thought there would be a time when I'd look at them in a different light.

Luna's father nods at the cop before coming our way. He runs his hand through his hair, scrubbing forward and back. "Chad'll be arrested for his outstanding warrants, and it's doubtful he'll be granted bail with his history of running."

Luna sits up, no longer shaking like a leaf. "Do I have to make a formal statement or press charges?"

Joe gives her a sorrowful smile. "You don't have to, but I wish you would at least get something on record in case he's ever an issue again."

Luna kicks her foot out. "If he does, these have his name on them."

He blows out a breath, glancing at the nighttime sky.

Luna snorts. "I'm kidding, Dad. I'll go down there tomorrow and talk to the police about what happened."

Joe looks instantly relieved. "They're taking him to the hospital to get checked out before he heads down to the county jail for processing. You," Joe says, looking directly at me, "take her home and make sure she gets some rest."

"Yes, sir."

"Take care of her," he tells me.

"I will. I promise," I reply.

He's trusting me with his child. Although she's fully grown and took down a whole-ass man, he's asking me to take care of her.

"Can we go now?" Luna asks me.

I place my arms under her legs and lift her. She doesn't let go of me as I jump down from the tailgate, holding on tight. "We'll get you home and tucked into bed."

"Stay with me tonight," she whispers against my neck.

"I'll stay with you as long as you need," I reply, knowing I'd stay forever if she asked me to.

24

LUNA

I OPEN MY EYES, SQUINTING FROM THE SUNLIGHT. MY body hurts as I stretch, and all the memories from last night come flooding back to me.

I lied when I pretended like I wasn't terrified. I was. When you're attacked, if you're not scared, you're a complete moron. But another part of me took over, going into overdrive, and acting instead of thinking. If I'd had a moment to think, I probably would've frozen, and the situation would've ended very differently.

Nevin rolls over, exposing his torso with the sheet lying across his bottom half. He looks so peaceful. It's hard to believe all the things he's been through in his life. He seems to have let go of some of his anger, easily fitting in with my family and realizing his past doesn't need to follow him into his future.

"Hey," he whispers and stretches, flexing all of his muscles. And there are a lot of them too.

He's still thin, but he's been gaining more weight since he got out. And if my grandmother has anything to do with it, he'll be bulked out in no time.

"Hey," I whisper back.

He reaches over, hauling me the few feet until I'm tucked against his side and my head is on his chest. "You okay?" he asks.

I place my palm against his pec, listening to the slow and steady beat of his heart. "I'm good."

"How are you, really?"

I peer up, meeting his green eyes. "I'm really okay. I promise. He's behind bars now, so I can stop looking over my shoulder, and you don't have to watch over me either."

His face tightens, and a darkness fills his eyes for the briefest of moments. "I'm glad you're safe."

"Me too."

His fingers trace a path up and down my spine, moving slowly and lightly. "Guess we can get back to normal."

"Yeah."

I hate the idea of what normal used to be like, though.

I never thought I'd like having someone else in my place. Someone other than my sister, that is. But having Nevin around has been better than nice. He's a calming force to me, and the fact that he's learning how to cook is a bonus.

"Nevin," I whisper.

"Yeah?"

I push myself up on my elbow and look down at his face. "I know you've said no before, but…" I stop and swallow, nervous for him to reject me again. "Do you think you'd want to move in with me? I mean, if you don't want to do it as a couple, maybe just as friends, at least."

He slides his hand down to the dip right above my ass. "You still want me to?"

I chew on my lip, wondering how I'm going to pretend not to be hurt when he shoots me down again. "Of course, but I don't want to pressure you."

He reaches up with his other hand, cupping my cheek. "There's nowhere else I'd rather be, Lu."

I release my breath, relieved. "Good." I smile, feeling like a weight has been lifted off my shoulders.

He brushes his thumb against my cheek as his green eyes soften. "But I don't want to be friends."

My heart sinks, and all the warm and fuzzies I had a moment ago vanish. "What?"

"If I'm moving in, I want everything. All of it. You. Me. Us. Everything I thought I could never and would never have."

My belly flips at his declaration. "You want it all?"

He nods. "Everything."

My heart hammers in my chest. "Guess there's no more going slow, huh?"

He smiles, and the way he does it makes my body

warmer than the sun on any summer day. "Not with you, babe."

"I'm okay with it that," I say, and I'm not lying. I don't want to take things slow. He's lost enough time, and I've wasted more than my share.

When you know, you know.

"I didn't think it was possible for anything to happen so quickly, but I love you, Lu."

My heart skips a beat. "You love me?" I whisper.

"I love you," he repeats, curling his fingers into my hair. "I realized it last night when I thought something happened to you. I don't know what I'd do if—"

I place my finger against his lips. "Shh. Don't say it. I'm fine," I assure him.

He smiles behind my fingertip.

I swallow, bracing myself for words I've never spoken to anyone except my closest friends and family. "I love you too, Nevin."

"You do?" He looks genuinely surprised. "Really?"

"What's not to love? You're sweet but still grumpy. You're protective but not overbearing. You don't care about my crazy past."

"Babe, I got the top spot for crazy pasts."

I laugh, unable to stop smiling at him. "You sure do, but none of that matters anymore."

He pulls me down on top of him until we're face-to-face. "For the first time in my life, I'm excited about the future, Luna. I don't think you understand what that means."

"The future is always supposed to be a good thing."

He shakes his head. "It never has been for me, but you gave that to me."

My vision blurs, and my nose tickles. A feeling I don't get often. "I didn't do anything."

Nevin cups my face in the palms of his hands, staring at me with those beautiful green eyes. "You gave me hope when I thought there was none. You did everything to make finding my way again in life easy. You showed me kindness when you didn't have to, and even when I made it hard. You showed me compassion and understanding when no one else would have had the patience. You didn't give up on me or judge me for who I was or what I've done, babe. You did everything, and for that, I'll be forever grateful that you were in my life."

"Were?" I tease, rolling my eyes.

"Babe, are. You are. I'm talking about someday when I'm lying on my deathbed, thinking about the life I lived. Even if you aren't in my life anymore, I'll think back on this time with only great memories and thankfulness."

"Shoot," I say, trying to shake my head, but his grip is too solid. "You already have us ending before we even begin."

"You can't cage a wild thing forever," he says before tipping his head forward, eyes trained on mine, and pressing his lips against my mouth.

"Are we breaking up?" I ask, not sure what the hell he's talking about.

"No. Of course not."

"Then what the hell with the can't cage a wild thing forever?"

"Fuck if I know, but it sounded good, didn't it? I'm only quoting you."

"Yeah, but stop being cute. It hurts my head." I close my eyes, letting myself get lost in the warmth of his body, the safety of his embrace, and the hardness of his kiss.

This is what I've always wanted.

Someone who understands me and doesn't try to change me. Someone who won't box me in or try to domesticate me in ways I never can be trained.

I don't want a traditional life, and I know with Nevin, nothing will ever be normal.

It couldn't be.

EPILOGUE

LUNA

NEVIN STARES UP AT THE LIGHTS ON THE STRIP, HIS mouth hanging open and at a complete loss for words.

I squeeze his arm tighter, moving closer to his side. "You like it?"

He lifts his arm, throwing it over my shoulder. "It's so...so..."

"I know," I say, watching his face as he takes it all in.

"I've never seen anything like it. Pictures don't do it justice."

"I knew you'd like it."

He wasn't sold on the idea of a vacation, but when I mentioned Vegas, it only took a little arm-twisting. Ever since we got off the plane, he hasn't stopped. We've barely been in our room because he wants to see everything, which is impossible in only four short days.

"It's magical," he says softly, his face aglow from the lights. "You know what we should do?"

"Elope," I joke.

He glances down. "Yeah."

My eyes widen, and my belly flips. It's been one year since we moved in together. One year since he told me he loved me and I admitted the same. Life has been good. No. Not good. It's been great.

"Are you serious?" I ask him.

His arm is gone a second later, and he drops down in front of me on one knee. "I don't have a ring yet, but Luna Gallo, will you do me the honor of marrying me?"

I blink, my mouth hanging open, trying my best to ignore the people around us who are now pointing and talking about what's happening.

"I love you more than anything in the world, and I want you to be mine forever."

I stare at him, my vision blurring from the tears. But I have no fear. No uncertainty in my heart. I want this man. I want him to be mine and for me to be his.

"Yes!" I throw my arms around him, kneeling on the pavement with him. "Yes, Nevin. I'll marry you."

He grabs my face, smashing his mouth against mine and kissing me deeper than he ever has before.

When he pulls back, I stare into his green eyes, seeing nothing but my future. "But promise me something," I whisper.

"What?" he says, his eyes searching mine.

"That we can redo the ceremony in front of our friends and family when Ian gets home."

"You want to marry me twice?"

"I do," I tell him, never having felt so sure of anything in my life.

"Anything you want. But now we have a big decision."

"What?"

"Elvis or something more traditional?"

I laugh, thinking he was going somewhere else with that question. "We're in Vegas. Elvis, baby."

He laughs, pulling me in again and hugging me tighter. I lean into him, closing my eyes, and I kiss him, knowing our future is filled with endless possibilities.

TRACE CALDO HAS ALWAYS BEEN a restless soul. He's the life of the party, strikingly handsome, and a lady killer.

It's going to take a strong woman to tame the wild bachelor, but don't worry, she won't make anything easy for Mr. Trace Caldo and he's loving every minute of the hunt.

TAP HERE or visit menofinked.com/torch to get your copy and don't miss a page of Gallo fun!

Dear Gallo Girl,

Thank you for your patience while waiting for the release of Luna and Nevin's story. I'd be lying if I said it was an easy one to write. I probably have fifty different versions started and saved in the depths of my laptop. Sometimes Ian lives, sometimes he dies. Other versions don't have Nevin in them at all and Ian's barely there. Some are more serious. Some more sad. But none of them felt right until this version.

I struggled with depression since we left our home in sunny Florida and moved back to the snowy north. I didn't think the weather and the stress of the move would affect me so much, but they did. Depression isn't something that's easy to get rid of. I struggled all winter, adding more pressure with trying to type just the right words. It didn't matter what I wrote—I hated every single word of it.

Thankfully, the feeling passed. I met with a therapist weekly, meditated, relaxed, binged everything possible, and did stuff for me to try to find my joy again. And it worked. I dug into an old draft I had written over the winter, this one you're reading now, and decided it felt right.

In all honesty, it was the version where Ian died at the beginning. My alpha readers were pissed too. They had a fit that I killed off Ian. I thought about their feedback and knew they were right. Ian had to live. He was too good of a guy, and maybe someday (a long way away), he might get his own book too.

It was great to spend time with the Gallos. They always brighten my day, making me feel like I'm part of something bigger. I hope spending time with them helped to put a smile on your face as much as it did mine.

I know this might not be my spiciest book. My brain couldn't handle it right now. I needed something that made me feel good and gave me the warm and fuzzies. I think I accomplished this, and I hope it felt like coming home.

Thank you for always being amazing and being part of my life. Even on my darkest days, I know I have a community of friends who want nothing but the best for me.

I'm honored to have you in my life.

And the good news? I feel like I'm back. I feel more confident and happier. I'm excited to write the next book in the Men of Inked series too. It's been a while since I've felt like me and nothing has ever felt so good.

I hope you're ready for Trace's story in TORCH... It's going to be a wild ride.

Love Always — Chelle Bliss

MEN OF INKED HEATWAVE #11

Trace Caldo has always been a restless soul. He's the life of the party, strikingly handsome, and a lady killer.

It's going to take a strong woman to tame the wild bachelor, but don't worry, she won't make anything easy for Mr. Trace Caldo and he's loving every minute of the hunt.

TAP HERE or visit menofinked.com/torch to get your copy and don't miss a page of Gallo fun!

OPEN ROAD SERIES

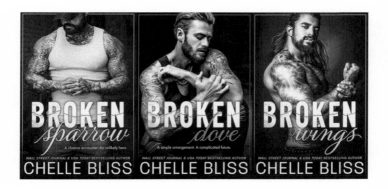

Book 1 - Broken Sparrow (Morris)
Book 2 - Broken Dove (Leo)
Book 3 - Broken Wings (Crow)

ABOUT THE AUTHOR

I'm a full-time writer, time-waster extraordinaire, social media addict, coffee fiend, and ex-history teacher. *To learn more about my books, please visit menofinked.com.*

Want to stay up-to-date on the newest
Men of Inked release and more?
Join my newsletter at *menofinked.com/news*

Join over 10,000 readers on Facebook in Chelle Bliss Books private reader group and talk books and all things reading. Come be part of the family!

See the Gallo Family Tree

Where to Follow Me:

facebook.com/authorchellebliss1

instagram.com/authorchellebliss

bookbub.com/authors/chelle-bliss

goodreads.com/chellebliss

tiktok.com/@chelleblissauthor

amazon.com/author/chellebliss

twitter.com/ChelleBliss1

pinterest.com/chellebliss10

Original Men of Inked Series

Have you read the Original Men of Inked series?

Join Joe, Mike, Izzy, Thomas, and Anthony as they search for their true love and a happily ever after.

See where your favorite series started!

Please visit *menofinked.com/inked-series* to learn more and start your next favorite read!

TO LEARN MORE ABOUT THE
MEN OF INKED HEATWAVE SERIES VISIT
MENOFINKED.COM/HEATWAVE

Made in the USA
Thornton, CO
07/28/22 12:49:50

0a9f688a-f4f2-47cf-a49c-cd0ac3705235R01